NANA

MARK TOWSE

D & T
PUBLISHING

I am dedicating this debut novella to my mum, Jennifer Syder. In my short career to date, she has read close to everything I've put out there, enduring all sorts of dark and weird journeys. She's my first reader and editor, very reasonably priced (free), incredibly responsive, eagle-eyed, and I couldn't do it without her. Please note, there is an exclusive contract in place that restricts her from taking on work that isn't mine.
Love you, Mum x

Nana: A term of endearment used in some countries for one's Grandma. Some say the title is derived from the Italian word for Grandmother, Nonna. Another theory is that it stems from the word Nanny, i.e., someone who takes care of children.

CLEMENTINE

SOMEWHERE IN ENGLAND — SATURDAY, 1ST SEPTEMBER 2018.

THERE'S the usual heaviness in the air that Clementine has come to expect over the years. It's a large room with a high ceiling, and even though very minimal, it feels quite claustrophobic on occasions like these. Always a stickler for detail, she carefully adjusts each of the chairs at the tables so they sit as close to perfectly parallel to each other as the naked eye can manage. Using the flowers cut from her garden this morning, she fills each of the small vases set atop the eight tables of the community centre. Finally, running her hand across each of the tables, checking for dust, she makes her way to the stage area to collect the books.

As she hikes her foot up onto the stage area, her right leg gives a ferocious crack that brings her to the ground, forcing her into a half-straddled position across the ten-inch wooden step. She sighs loudly, counts to ten, and grimaces as she pushes herself up. Blunt dentures cut through her lip as though it's a ripened fruit, and warm dark liquid begins running down her chin. She begins to cry, not just for herself but for the events that will shortly unfold. The others have hardened to it, most of them anyway, but she still gets nightmares.

Back to her feet, she brushes herself down and clambers over the step on all fours like an animal, wondering why she didn't take the side ramp. *No spring chicken anymore—more like an out-of-date turkey.* She notices a new flap of skin hanging down from her shoulder and tries patting it back in place, but it refuses to fall back into formation. A strange and garbled noise of desperation leaves her lips as she gingerly continues to the table next to the microphone. She used to love being on stage; it made her feel as though she was someone special—as if she were holding the crowd in the palm of her hand and taking them on a journey. The prospect of singing now, though, fills her with bittersweet nostalgia.

Opening the box, mindful of her shoulder, she runs her hand across the gold embossed lettering of one of the books. She lifts it out to find it heavier than she remembers, but it's a bad day for her today; she feels particularly weak and fragile. It's times like this that she wants to get into bed and not wake up, and even the idea of slipping into death gives her a pleasant prickle across her skin.

She grabs four of the books and slides herself down the step, placing the stack in the centre of the first table. As she gets on with the business of delivering to each one, the face of her dead husband, Alf, flashes in her head, and she's hit with a pang of sadness. Even after all this time, the pain is still raw, like a red-hot poker working at her insides. A lot of it is a blur, but she can still remember how weighty the knife felt as she began to work it across his neck.

The tables are ready.

She makes her way to the door with the empty box, her leg still offering pulses of dull pain with each step. She turns, taking a moment to admire her handiwork, her finger hovering over the light switch. Little pleasures, she thinks to herself, managing a small smile.

At home, she will run a bath and light some candles. Perhaps she'll have a little snooze.

It's going to be a late night.

ALEX

ALEX BENDS over to pick up the orange bag of newspapers, noticing his mum smiling at him through the bay window of the lounge. Tonight, she's cooking chips for tea, from scratch, not the crappy frozen ones from the supermarket. He already has his evening planned out. After the paper round, he'll take Charlie for her obligatory around the block walk, eat as many chips as he can, laced with copious amounts of salt and ketchup of course, and then sit down and spend quality time on the PlayStation until his dad gets home. After tea, he'll no doubt be roped into watching that silly police series his dad likes, and they'll all curl up with Charlie on the sofa.

His mum mouths something at him, pointing to the sky, and he nods as he throws the bag of papers across his shoulders and picks up his bike from the driveway. He's had a good run with the weather of late, but today looks ominous with a blanket of dull grey above. His mum offered to take him in the car to save him from a possible drenching, but this feels like it is something he should be doing alone. Besides, it would only mean having to listen to that God-awful old-fashioned music that she insists on singing along to.

For just over a week, he's been doing this round. It's an easy one mostly, people keeping to themselves, and for the most part, he gets away without any boring chit-chat. Some people even scurry away when they see him coming, dropping what they're doing, be it washing their cars or mowing their lawns, waiting for him to pass before popping their heads out again. If the folk of Newhaven Crescent did that, it would be the easiest money of his life.

He turns into Argyle Street and leaves his bike leaning on the street sign. The weather seems to be keeping everyone inside, and that suits him fine. It doesn't take long at all to deliver to the thirty or so houses, and he's already planning his strategy for the online war campaign tonight. Collecting his bike, he rides down to Plymouth Street, avoiding the rickety fence on the corner that imprisons the hound from Hell. He sometimes forgets, in a world of his own, and the shock as the dog throws itself against the fence sets his nerves on edge for some time. Not today, though. He's ready for it.

The bark from the dog is just as loud, and he sees the frenzied teeth snapping at him through the wooden slats. He's often wondered what the dog would do if it got through—if it's just looking for a cuddle, a bit of attention perhaps, or if it would quite happily chew his balls off.

"Fuck you, Cujo!"

It's a pleasant street, the posh part of town; well-manicured gardens with sprinklers, nice cars, big houses, and it's even got a park. Not the cheap plastic equipment that guarantees friction burns, but a proper snazzy steel slide and swing set. There's a zip-line, too. Richard Brannigan once pushed him so hard that he flipped and landed face down in bark, right next to white dog poo. Someone took a picture, he can't remember who now, but it ended up on the internet with the tagline, 'Spot the difference.'

He gets a couple of polite smiles as he moves from house to house, people pottering around, but it's another quick and easy one. The same goes for the next street. He's making excellent time, but that means nothing. It's time to make his way to Newhaven Crescent now. The hairs on the back of his neck are already beginning to bristle as he prays the ominous clouds will keep the freaks and their leaky skin indoors.

IVY

She dabs some foundation across her face, smooths it out, and follows up with a thick application of blusher. She studies her reflection in the antique mirror with sadness. In addition to the age spots, small red lesions have started to appear on both cheeks, and they're getting harder to disguise with make-up. There are half a dozen large welts on the back of her legs that arrived in unison a few weeks ago and are causing quite a lot of discomfort. They weep relentlessly, and she can't leave the house without padding and long pants anymore. Some of her hair fell out in the shower this morning, too. It's getting on top of her, making her edgy and short-tempered. It's the oldest she ever remembers looking.

Spraying a few squirts of the atomiser onto her fingers, she dabs her hand across her neck and underneath her chin. It was George's favourite, always said it smelt like an orchard on a breezy summer day. She runs her fingers across the photograph pinned to the mirror, tracing his smile and hearing his laughter in her head. Moving her fingers further along, she runs them down the chain of the silver necklace that hangs over the top right-hand corner of the frame, letting them come to rest on the small globe pendant.

She feels it coming, inflating in her chest like a big balloon. Flatulence has become an unbearable blemish on her dignity, and it's becoming a lot worse of late. This one's a big one, and it's continuing to turn her insides over. Lifting her right buttock an inch from the stool, she screws her face up and releases. For all the build-up, it's a rather anti-climactic flatness, not like the rip-roaring one she made in the grocery store yesterday that set the little girl off laughing. Still overpowering, though—possibly the worst one yet in terms of assaulting the smell sense—as though someone has laced a mound of rotting flesh with perfume.

Cursing under her breath, she pushes herself to her feet and opens the bedroom window. The cool breeze falls against her cheek as she returns to the chair, determined to make herself as presentable as possible for the night ahead.

The soft bristles of the make-up brush disturb a loose piece of skin that she's been having issues with, and she curses and puts her finger on it, trying to guide it back in place. It slides against the moist and weeping layer of skin beneath but refuses to hold. Keeping some pressure applied to the centre of the skin piece, she pulls out the top drawer of the dresser and rakes through the many containers of make-up and bandages until she finds the tube of superglue. It's the same brand George swore by. She'll never use anything different; it's like an act of honour. She unscrews the top and squeezes a little, guiding the glue around the edge of the skin before squishing it firmly back in place and beginning a countdown from thirty. It's an effort to raise herself from the stool, and she grimaces at the crack of her hips and the pain that shoots through her knobbly fingers as she puts her weight on the dresser. Through the gap in the net curtains, she observes the thick blanket of clouds in the distance and lets out a small shudder of impatient excitement. On the next street, she can see Alex approaching on his bike. Such a wonderful boy, so full of youth and vigour.

The oven bell sounds. Perfect timing.

JOAN

JOAN STANDS an inch behind the net curtains, breathing excitedly as the boy leans his bike against the lamppost. There's a crackle in her throat, though, and she can feel something catching with each laboured gasp. Quickly pulling the tissue from her sleeve, she begins to hack into it, eventually producing a thick dark globule of nastiness. *He's coming! He's coming*! She begins to hop from one foot to the next, upping the tempo until he's halfway down the path.

Staggering to the front door, she swings it open. "Hi, Alex," she says rather loudly, heart pounding and a bead of sweat running down her forehead. She can feel a little bit of wee running down her right leg, too.

"Oh, hi," he mumbles back solemnly, reaching into the orange bag for the paper. As he looks up, he eyes the tissue in her left hand and lets out a little shudder of disgust.

Attempting to hide it behind her back, Joan catches her hand on her hip, and the sudden bolt of arthritic pain causes her to release the tissue. They both watch it fall to the beige shag pile carpet, landing with the glistening darkness on full display. There's an awkward silence, a stand-off of sorts, and they both continue staring at the tissue as it unfurls slowly into an even bigger spectacle of disgust. Finally, as if in synchronisation, they lift their heads and make eye contact. Joan smiles and lets out a little giggle. Alex smiles back but feels his stomach turning over.

Letting out a long groan as she bends over to retrieve the tissue, Alex notes the rather large and hideous knobbly dark brown lump on her scalp. It has three heads and a flurry of pitch-black hairs emerging from the largest one in the centre of the cluster. He begins to feel quite dizzy, his vision now monopolised by this otherworldly formation, everything else swimming out of focus. Part of him wants to reach out and touch it to see if it is soft or hard, while the other part wants to throw up his lunch. He's no longer in the mood for chips.

With another pained groan, Joan manages to stand and indiscreetly throw the tissue behind her.

"You don't want to get old, Alex," she mutters, reaching towards the top of his head with her free hand. Alex clenches his teeth and screws his eyes tightly shut as the hand makes contact and begins to rake at his hair in a sideways motion. Having his head patted and hair dishevelled is his least favourite thing in the world, but the sensation of the old lady's sticky hand all over this scalp makes him want to scream.

Old people freak him out in a big way, make him feel unbearably uncomfortable. They're like an alien species to him, full of weird ways—and the smell—well, it's like someone has taken a bag of scented candy and pissed all over it.

"How was school today?" she asks, still fondling at his hair.

"Fine." It was the same boring questions every day.

"Do you want to come in for soda?"

"No, I best be getting on home. Looks like rain."

"Does it?" she says, looking up to the dark clouds that are beginning to roll in. "Oh, yes. You best come in then—out of the rain."

"It's not raining yet."

"But it will. Look at the clouds."

"I know. I just told you that. Look, I best be going."

"I'll pay you. To come in, I mean."

"No, thanks. Here's the paper, lady."

"It's Joan," she snaps, reaching towards it.

As soon as she grabs it, he turns and walks back down the path. "Bye." *You crazy bitch.*

"Bye, Alex. See you soon. Looks like rain, eh?"

She watches him as he starts up the pathway to Harry at number three, the way his lovely brown hair catches in the breeze, and the way he skips along like a gazelle, as though it was nothing. Lifting the hand that she patted him with to her nostrils, she inhales deeply, enjoying the tingles it sends across her body. Another little bit of wee begins to dribble down her leg.

HARRY

Harry opens the door and performs the same trick as always, pretending to masturbate until his hand opens in an explosion of fake ejaculate. Smoothly, he snaps the paper out of Alex's hand as the final part of the act. He's a tall and gangly fellow, and his face is so thin and pale that it looks to Alex as though there's only a single layer of skin stretched across his skull. Thick black hairs, at least half-an-inch long, emerge from over-sized nostrils, and Alex counts only six hairs on the top of the man's head. It's the huge boil, though, on the side of the old man's neck that makes Alex feel queasiest. It's leaking thick dark pus that is spilling over to the inside of the man's shirt.

"Have you been laid recently, Alex?"

"No, sir."

"Shame. If I were your age, I'd be getting as much fanny as I could, lad."

"I'm twelve."

"That's alright; you're just a late starter." Harry extends his right arm and begins to thrust his mid-section at the air in front, grunting like a pig with every swing of his hips.

"During the war, they used to call me gunner Morton. Ask me why."

"Why?"

"Because of the amount of seamen I shot." he replies, peppering the air with invisible bullets from his crotch and making remarkably realistic machine gun sounds. "Do you get it?"

"Yeah."

"Seaman. Ejaculate. Yeah?"

"Yeah," Alex replies, giving him a half-smile.

"Come here, son, I've got some advice for you," Harry says, beckoning him with the longest finger Alex has ever seen.

Alex takes one small step forward.

"Closer, boy. I won't bite."

Alex takes another step forward.

"Closer still. Look, I'm not going to grab your disco stick if that's what you're worried about."

"I wasn't, but I am now."

Impatiently, Harry takes a step forward and bends down until his nose hairs threaten to tickle Alex's ear. "Thick thighs make the best earmuffs," he whispers and begins to cackle.

"Bye then. Thanks for the advice," Alex says, quickly turning and marching to number four. The first time he delivered to the street, he made the mistake of accepting an invitation inside from Harry. The coffee table was littered with pornographic magazines, like the ones on the top shelf of the news-stands. As he sipped from a flat can of soda, Harry proceeded to take him through the ones on the top of the pile, pointing out all the naughty bits and describing them in a way that took away all of the mystery. Some of the pages were stuck together, too.

"Be careful with her at number four, Alex. She'll crush you to death," Harry says, giving a final grunt and pelvic sway before closing the door behind him, whispering "wasted youth" under his breath.

JANET

JANET IS STANDING in the doorway, arms like Christmas hamper meat, impossibly folded into each other. The first time he saw her, he was petrified. She reminds Alex of a cross between a sumo wrestler and a sergeant major. After their first meeting, he had a dream about her chasing him down the street, wearing a big white nappy, and barking at him to give her ten.

"Take no notice of that filthy old pervert, Alex."

Alex gives a salute and hands the paper across. It's kind of a thing. She returns the salute and affords him a smile.

As she subsequently reaches for the paper, she slides a clammy arm around the back of his neck and brings him into her bosom. His legs buckle under the weight, and he knows he's likely to have nightmares tonight about being suffocated. There's a disturbing black vein that runs down the lady's throat, too. *Fuck, did it just—it did, it fucking moved!* He's never seen it move before, but today it's wriggling up and down her throat like a worm.

"What is it, sonny?" Janet asks rather sternly, reaching for her throat. There's a rumble of thunder above.

"N—nothing," he replies, but he can't take his eyes off it.

"It's just age," she replies awkwardly, tapping at her throat until the blackness disappears. "Nothing for you to worry your pretty little head about," she adds, squeezing him into her cleavage again.

"If you say so."

Beneath the veil of perfume and acrid sweat, he can smell something much more unpleasant but can't put his finger on it."

"How's life for you anyway, friend?"

"Fine, I guess."

"You've got to grab it by the balls," she says, pointing towards the crotch of his pants, momentarily making him think she might reach for them.

"Okay," he replies weakly.

She leans in and inhales the top of his head. "Ah, the smell of the young," she says. "Time for a soda? You promised last time."

"No, but definitely next time."

"Suit yourself." She grabs the paper out of his clutch and gives him a nudge with her behind that sends him stumbling sideways.

"Can't stand chatting all day. Off you fuck, then."

HE's longing to be back at home, sitting behind his PlayStation and away from the old. Two more weeks of doing the round, though, and he'll be able to buy the new Dragonland release. He'll be the envy of the school.

YOU'VE GOT THIS, *Alex. They're fucking crazy, but they're human. Just.*

HE GETS a lucky run with the next couple of houses, and he knows he's always on a winner with number seven, the one belonging to Micky the Mime. Micky does this thing at the window, pressing against it with his white-gloved hands as though he's pretending to get out, screaming a silent scream. Today is no different. Alex manages to avoid eye contact.

No such luck with the next one. He's already spotted Geoff in the door-way, the nutter with the toolbox full of toenails. He's shaking it over his right shoulder like a bizarre maraca.

GEOFF

"HI, GEOFF."

Geoff is a small olive-skinned man with eyes pointing in different directions. Alex never knows which one to look at, so he alternates his gaze frequently between the two. He's hairless apart from two bushy grey eyebrows that sit on his forehead like obese caterpillars. Their exchanges are always memorable.

Geoff gives a shake of the lunchbox. "If you guess how many I've got in here, Alex, I'll give you twenty pounds."

"Crikey, I have no idea. I'll say three hundred and six."

Geoff shakes the box again as thunder rumbles around them. His lips twist into a frenzied smile, and his eyes widen.

"Well?" Alex prompts.

"Well, what?" Geoff replies, eyebrows squishing together in an audible bristle.

"How many are in there?"

"How many what?"

"Toenails in the box."

"I have no fucking idea, kid. What's it got to do with you?"

"You just asked me."

"Asked you what?"

"Never mind. Here's your paper."

"Thanks, kid."

"Can I ask you a question, Geoff?"

Geoff nods, sporting his inane smile and shaking the box again.

"Why do you keep your toenails in a box?"

"Oh, they're not my toenails, kid. That would be weird."

Alex walks away, shaking his head, noting the rapidly fading light as the first spot of rain splashes on the bridge of his nose. He escapes from contact with the residents of the next few, but Edith is waiting for him at number eighteen, sporting a blue rinse and wearing the cheeky little grin he's become accustomed to. Alex can tell she was most likely very pretty when she was younger; she still has a sparkle in her eyes and a decent figure for someone so ancient. Absolute nutcase, though. There's a saying his mum likes to use—crazier than a soup sandwich.

EDITH

"Boyfriend, you didn't bring me flowers?"

He remains silent.

"How do you expect to get to second base if you don't buy me flowers?"

"I've got a girlfriend, Edith."

"Ah, but she can't do what I can—betcha."

Half-heartedly, Alex extends the paper towards her, praying for her to take it so he can turn and leave. Instead, she wraps her bony fingers around his wrist and drags him forward until her face is only an inch from his. He hears the cough sweet rattling around as she moves her lips close to his ear. It's a smell that he knows will take some time to forget—a cocktail of eucalyptus and shit. "Come inside, and I'll blow a tune out of your little flute," she whispers.

"It's raining," he says. "I've got to get back."

She begins to laugh. "I'm just fooling with you, kid. But I do expect a birthday kiss tonight. Had my hair done special; do you like it?"

"Yes."

"What do you like about it?"

"It's—erm—very blue."

"Suits me perfectly then," she replies, following up with another dirty snigger. "Anyhow, tonight is going to be wild. Music, dancing, there's even going to be a talent show. I bet you've got loads of talents, haven't you, Alex?"

Sheepishly, he looks down towards the ground and cannot help but notice the large sores on the sides of Edith's legs.

"Hideous, aren't they?"

"Sorry, I just—"

"You don't want to get old, Alex. Best leave this world early with your dignity," she says.

"Okay," he offers resignedly.

"Anything good in the news today?"

"I never read the papers really, just hand them out."

"Don't blame you, Alex. Death, crime, people going missing; the world is going crazy."

He almost sniggers at her comment. What was the word for that?

"I like being here, insulated away from all that razzmatazz," she adds, fondly patting her door frame. "Peaceful. Nobody bothers us, and we play by our own rules. Anyhow, I'll be looking for you tonight. Don't think you can get away without a smooch."

Relief washes over him as she takes hold of the paper. He performs a quick about-turn and marches back down the path to number thirteen. The curtains twitch, but the door stays closed. Home straight now, he thinks to himself. He eyes shadows behind the dirty yellow nets of the next house, but once again, he breathes a sigh of relief as he escapes contact.

One more to go, but it's the house he's rather excited about.

It a pretty building, sitting proudly at the end of the cul de sac. The front garden, though, is over-stuffed with statues and colourful knick-knacks that cheapen it a little. One of the concrete figures reminds Alex of Harry at number three. It's a leprechaun smoking a cigar; its tiny hand curled around a very small spout that sprays water onto the plants beneath. Out of all the gargoyles and twisted faces, it's the Harry look-a-like that disturbs him the most.

The pie on the welcome mat, just as promised, prompts his stomach to give out a groan of approval. Alex likes Ivy the best out of the oldies, certainly finding her the sweetest and kindest of the bunch. He opens the gate and performs a little skip down the path before sitting down under the porch and scooping up the silver fork that sits beside the dish. Another groan emerges as he digs it into the crust, allowing the rich red fruit to spill across the pastry. He quickly picks up the note and reads the scrawl across it: *Alex, enjoy your cherry pie.*

The rain turns heavy just as he places the fork in his mouth, but he's not thinking about the ride home. Right now, it's just him and the pie. He's never really taken the time to savour the taste of something properly, but this pie demands full attention. In his mouth, the warm crust gives way to a fluffier pastry and an explosion of fruit that provides a heady cocktail of sugary perfection. It tastes so good that it induces a small giggle from Alex before he takes the next mouthful. Each bite tastes as good as the first as he shovels the pie in and lets the exquisiteness slide down his throat, filling his belly with wholesome warmth. He licks his fingers and runs his tongue around the side and bottom of the white pie dish to make sure no crumb is left. Even with a full belly, there is still a sense of disappointment at finishing. It's getting late, though, and it doesn't look like the rain is going to stop anytime soon.

He tries to push himself up, but his arms suddenly feel quite floppy. With a huge effort, he manages to stand, but a wave of dizziness makes him reach out for the bricks. His legs feel heavy, as do his eyelids, and there's a blurriness to his vision.

He eyes the road ahead, which appears much longer and narrower than before.

BENJAMIN

HE CAN FEEL the stickiness of the sores on his back, but it's the one on the back of his neck that seems to be leaking the most. It's itchy, too, but through the rubber of the gas mask, he can't quite get to it. Turning his attention back to the paperboy, he begins to slap at the wound until it becomes numb.

His breathing is heavy and excited, and it's getting hot inside the mask, but that's the way he likes it. He's worn it many times before during what he coins his self-care sessions. There's a stir in his groin area that sets him thinking about the evening's proceedings, but he snaps himself out of it and gets back to the mission at hand.

Rain beats down hard against the window, and Benjamin almost feels sorry for the kid as he watches him launch into a run, the empty orange bag above his head. It's a great start; the kid is fast, real fast, but it isn't long before his legs buckle, and he's sent sprawling face down into the wet tarmac. The legs perform a quick jig and settle to a slow twitch until finally, the kid is motionless.

In his element, Benjamin reaches for the walkie-talkie. "Man down."

He takes off the mask and picks up another matchstick, cursing as the glue spills over the edge onto his fingers. The matchstick shakes vigorously as he brings it across to the bough of the model boat, and only on the third attempt does it find its rightful spot. Two months he's been working on the piece, and it's almost finished. It would have been done a lot quicker if it wasn't for rheumatoid arthritis that's returned with a bite.

OLLY, JENNY, AND FRANK'S PLACE.

"We're leaving soon. Have you packed your little case, Olly?"

"Why are you speaking to me like a toddler? And I'm not going by the way. Nana stinks!"

"Hey, that's your dad's mum you're talking about. Besides, it's only one night, Olly. Your dad and I need to talk."

Olly looks away in disgust, throwing his hands behind his head and leaning the chair on its hind legs. "But Jenny, I'm twelve now. I'll be alright on my own!"

"I'm your mother, don't call me Jenny. And we already talked about this. A couple of hours here and there is fine, but you're too young to be left on your own overnight."

"What does Dad say?"

"Your dad agrees with me," she says, removing the pie from the oven.

"Of course, he does. You've taken his balls and hidden them in a jar somewhere."

"Olly!" Jenny places the pie carefully on the cooking tray, hands beginning to tremble.

"How is Roger, these days, anyway?"

She takes a step back, inhaling deeply. "We discussed that, Olly. It's for your dad and me to work through."

"I just don't understand how you could do it, Mum? Especially after Dad being so ill."

"Stop it, Olly," she pleads. "You know nothing about it. You know how happy I was when your dad recovered, but ever since, he's been spending all his time with his mum. It's unhealthy. I call to ask where he is, and he's always fixing a faucet or mowing one of the lawns for the weirdos down her street."

"Do you still love him?"

"He's different, Olly, like a stranger. I'm trying, but he's not making it easy. That's what tonight is about."

"You don't love me anymore either, do you?"

"That's simply not true. Olly, I adore you. You can't see that right now, I know, because you've always been so close to your dad, and you think less of me at the—"

"Did you do a sixty-niner?"

"Olly!" Her right eye is beginning to twitch.

"Is his wiener bigger than Dad's?"

"Enough!" she bellows, slamming her hands down so hard on the bench, the pie moves half an inch to the right.

The cry takes Olly by surprise, and he recoils, sending the chair off balance and plummeting backwards. He screws his eyes tightly shut in preparation for the impact, and sure enough, a sharp pain swells at the back of his head. There's an urge to cry, but he doesn't want to give her the pleasure.

Rushing across, still sporting the oven mitt, her anger is already beginning to recede, and she has to stifle a laugh at the sight of Olly's face turning bright red and his lips puckered in rage and embarrassment.

"Why do you hate us?" Olly spits, urgently pushing from the floor and stomping off, kicking at the air in front of the cat on the way past. Beatrice scowls and hisses, returning the contempt.

Jenny sighs as she reaches for the cooling tray from the cupboard. She carefully places the pie on top and grabs the kitchen bench, dropping her shoulders in resignation. A single tear rolls down her right cheek.

She curses the day Olly found the note while snooping for birthday presents. It was shoved in the middle of some bedding along with a photograph—a reminder for her that she still had something more to offer than being a cook, a piece of flesh, and even a punching bag on the rare occasions that she challenged his priorities. She's excited at the thought of a second chance with Roger. He sent her a text yesterday telling her he had left his wife; said he was staying at a cheap motel and was waiting for her. It used to feel like a dream when they first started talking about it, but a second chance seems within reach now. Olly will inevitably continue to hate her, but he'll eventually come round and hopefully understand one day. It's just a case of breaking the news to Frank, and a busy restaurant seems like the perfect setting. It won't be the meal he's expecting, though.

Olly sits on the bed and begins to cry, longing for the days before he found the letter when everything was normal—before Roger came along with his tidy black hair and blue eyes. He knows his dad is much older than his mum, but that was her choice. Anyway, he still looks great for his age, especially after what he's been through, and it's not fair that he should have to go through this. Wiping away the tears, he distracts himself with his iPad, playing one of his favourite games, 'The Living Dead.' Thoughts turn to his nana, and he begins to wonder if old people would move faster than normal if they were bitten and turned into zombies.

A message comes through on his phone from his friend, Luke, asking if he can play Fortnite on the Playstation. He replies, saying he needs to leave in thirty minutes to travel back to the Dark Ages. A sad face immediately comes back, followed by the word 'loser.'

The sound of gravel crunching beneath tyres usually fills Olly with excitement, but he knows Jenny will get to his dad first. The car door shuts, and he follows the sound of footsteps to the door. It's immediate, the urgent but muffled voice of his mother, no doubt pointing out how evil their son is. He wraps his arms around his legs and begins to rock, waiting for the thud of footsteps on the stairs. There's a brief exchange, and the voices stop. The first creak of the stairs sends a shiver down Olly's spine, and he squeezes himself even smaller.

The knock is gentle, though, and followed by his father's soft voice. "Olly." It means Jenny most likely hasn't followed behind, hands on her hips, ready to adjudicate proceedings.

"Come in."

The door opens, and his dad smiles and perches on the end of the bed. Olly breathes a sigh of relief. He knows her absence means only a gentle ticking off.

"I know. I'm sorry," Olly spits. "I just don't know why I can't stay here tonight."

"Maybe next year, son," Frank consoles, reaching out to fist bump.

Olly offers his fist in return, and as they mimic an explosion, his face cracks into a smile.

"Dad."

"Yes, son."

Olly looks into his eyes, frowning to encourage a serious answer. "What's going to happen?"

"You don't need to worry about it, son. Just know it's going to be okay."

"Mum laughed when I fell off the chair."

"I'm sure there was more to it, Olly," he replies.

"Well, yeah, maybe."

"Your mum is just going through a bit of a phase, Olly. I'm feeling it, too."

"I guess." He feels quite cheated at the response and lack of anger from his father. Lately, his dad seems flat, distant almost, and with what's going on with his mum, it's making him feel quite lonely.

"I do understand, Olly," Frank says, ruffling up his son's hair. It's something Olly hates, but he says nothing. "I guess it feels like Mum isn't in our corner at the moment, eh?"

"Maybe. Dad, what was your mum like—when you were a kid?"

Frank curls his lips, letting out a muted laugh. "Well, your nana was awesome to tell you the truth. Solid. Always welcoming, always inviting my friends in for drinks and food. She was always fighting my battles, too—you know, always putting me at number one." He lets out another little snicker. "Still does, I guess. They certainly don't make 'em like they used to, kidder."

"I just—"

"It's okay, son. Leave your mum to me. I'll sort it, okay?"

"Okay."

"We're leaving in five, alright? I'm just going to get a quick shower and change. Nana's looking forward to seeing you; she has something special planned tonight."

Soggy biscuits and gardening programmes are the first things that come to Olly's mind. An hour or two is doable, but a whole night at Nana's house seems like forever.

"Can I take my iPad or phone this time? Please, Dad, it's so boring there."

"Sorry, Olly. You know how Nana is about such modern contraptions. Besides, I told you, she has something planned."

"Like what?"

His dad shrugs. "Bingo?"

"Bingo? What the fuck is bingo?"

"Language, Olly! You know I don't like you using that word. It's just a game they play down at the community centre. Give it a chance, and you might like it." He offers a wink on the way out.

Olly collects underwear and socks from the cupboard and puts them in the case, sliding his phone between them. He lays his fleecy dressing gown across the top and angrily pulls across the zip. Picking up his iPad, he enters bingo into the search bar to bring up a list of grids that look like maths problems. *Fuck's sake.*

As he wheels the case through to the hallway, he hears his dad whistling in the shower and wonders what he has to be so happy about.

"You two almost ready?" his mother shouts from the hallway.

"No, I can't find my gas mask," Olly yells. It's been over a year since he was there, but the thought of his nana's house is already making him edgy. He can still remember the smell, like washing that's dried too quickly or cardboard that's been left out in the rain. It's even worse after dinner when Nana sits next to the fire and lets them rip. Something about the heat and the smell mixed, and he still can't get what happened last time out of his head. He's not sure he'll be able to look his nana in the eye.

"Come on; it won't be as bad as you think. And you have your favourite cherry pie to look forward to," Jenny shouts. She's wearing a blue dress and red shoes. Olly thinks she looks quite pretty, and he guesses Roger thinks that, too. He slinks down the stairs, pulling the case behind him, trying to make as much noise as possible.

"I'll be two minutes," Frank says, poking his head out the bedroom door. "By the time you get in the car, I'll be there."

Jenny offers to take the case from Olly, but he recoils, angrily slaking it over her right foot and scowling as the cold air hits. He opens the car boot and slides the case in, feeling quite victorious that he still has his phone in transit.

His mum opens the passenger door and carefully climbs in, pie dish in hand, grimacing as she lets herself fall into the seat. Flipping down the sun visor, she fluffs her hair a little and runs a finger over the dark shading under her right eye. "Be good for Nana, okay? I know it's not your preference, but she's looking forward to seeing you."

Olly turns towards the window and says nothing.

"Olly!"

"'Kay, okay," he grunts, studying his maudlin reflection. "Why do old people fart so much?"

"I don't think they all do, Olly," his mum replies.

"And why does Nana wear those tops, the ones that her boobs spill out from. It's embarrassing."

"Olly, you shouldn't be looking at your nana's boobs," his mum replies, unable to prevent a giggle.

"I'm not! God! That's disgusting! They're like half-full water balloons." *How can she laugh? She shouldn't be laughing.*

He kicks the back of the seat angrily, the question bouncing in his head, refusing to quit. "Do you love him?"

"Who?"

"Roger." *Not laughing now, are you?*

"Olly, I told you, this is grown-up stuff. It's not for—"

"I told Dad," he whispers. "About the letter and photo."

She turns to him, eyes wide and mouth partially open. "When?"

"A couple of days ago." Olly watches his dad shut the door behind him and nervously clasps his hands together. "He said he already knew and that it was going to be okay," he adds, offering a hopeful smile.

There's no change on his mother's face. Olly continues to clutch his hands together as he turns away from her gaze.

"All good?" his dad asks, remarkably chirpy as he opens the driver door.

"We're fine. We were just talking about Nana's boobs," Olly replies.

"Yikes," Frank says as he starts the engine.

"Dad."

"Yes, son."

"What's Nana's actual name?"

"You're kidding? You actually don't know?"

"No."

"It's Ivy."

"How old is she?"

"I've got a headache, Frank. Do you mind if we give tonight a miss? I think I need to lie down."

"Nonsense. Mum will have some headache tablets. She's got drawers full of painkillers and whatnot. Besides, we've got lots of stuff to discuss tonight, Jenny. All on the table."

NEWHAVEN CRESCENT

It's already dark as they pull into Newhaven Crescent, thunderous rain pounding on the car windows. Hairs on the back of Olly's neck make their presence known, warning of many hours of uncomfortable and stifling boredom to come. His mum turns to him, expressionless, and he returns the gaze. Guilt turns his stomach, but she always told him it was always best to be honest. Besides, his dad already knew anyway.

Why did she have to do it? Why aren't we good enough? Fucking Roger! He knows he's going to have to stop hating her one day, but it's far too early.

"It's a lovely little place this," Frank says. "A real community, like places used to be once upon a time."

Jenny grunts. She can't stand Frank's mum, the way she dotes on Frank to the verge of it being cringy. From the very beginning of their relationship, she always thought it odd, and even after fifteen years of marriage, his mother still gives Jenny the impression she isn't good enough for him. This place makes her feel weird, too, starchy and claustrophobic.

"Are you coming in?" Franks says to her as he pulls up the driveway.

"No, I'll stay in the car."

"Suit yourself. Come on, champ." Frank exits the car and walks around to the boot.

"Olly," Jenny mutters softly.

"Yeah?" He wraps his fingers around the handle.

Her eyes are watery, and she looks like she might begin to sob. "I love you, son." She leans over and kisses him on the cheek.

"Me too," he mumbles, not wanting his dad to overhear.

"Whatever happens, I always will," she says, dabbing her nose with the back of her hand. "Don't forget the pie."

Olly carefully takes it from her and gets out of the car to find his dad waiting with the case. "Anything to declare?" Frank asks.

"No, honest. They're all on my bedside table."

His dad leans in close, and they do the thing they do, staring into each other's eyes and frowning until one of them breaks. Olly's the first to go, as always. "You can check if you like," he spits before caving in and launching into a giggle.

"I trust you, son."

Through the window, Jenny watches them, an emptiness in the pit of her stomach at the closeness they share. She's painfully jealous of the connection that Frank has with her flesh and blood. It wasn't always like that. She and Olly used to be inseparable. The smug bastard flashes her a smile as he puts an arm around Olly and escorts him down the path.

The frosted glass door opens even before they're halfway down, and here comes Ivy, open-armed and age-defying boobs on show. She hugs each of them tightly before ushering them in, briefly glancing back to the car but offering no acknowledgement of Jenny as she shuts the door behind her. Jenny has wished the woman dead many times, but the bitch keeps hanging on.

It's just as Olly remembers it; gaudy green wallpaper hosting an array of weird art—twisted demonic faces clumsily painted with an array of red and yellow shades against black backgrounds. He remembers now; the nightmares they used to give him as a kid, misshapen faces hurtling towards him like kites in crosswinds.

"Your nana's choice in art is interesting," his dad comments, nudging his shoulder.

Olly smiles and runs a finger over the textured canvas, being careful not to lose the pie. *Not scary anymore.*

"No grubby fingerprints please, young Olly," Ivy says sternly.

"Sorry, Nana."

"Let me take that from you, boy."

"Sure, thanks."

"Time for a cuppa, Frank, before you go?" she asks, placing the pie on the counter.

"No thanks, Mum. The table's booked, and I don't want to be late."

"Lucky girl—your mum, Olly. Some people just don't realise a good thing until it's gone."

"Have you got any painkillers, Mum? Jenny's got one of her headaches."

Ivy sighs and shakes her head. "Too much going on inside her brain. Never trust a girl that gets a lot of headaches, Olly. It means her mind is elsewhere, fretting over things she has no business fretting over."

She stomps through to the kitchen mumbling something under her breath as she swings open the pantry door. The box she lifts out is huge, and she can barely see over it as she swings it around, slamming it onto the kitchen counter. Working the lid loose, she brings out a handful of packets. "Here, these are the best ones. In half an hour, she won't feel a thing."

"Swell. Thanks, Mum. Alright, Alex, you be good for Nana, okay?"

"Ah, he's a good lad. We'll have fun tonight, for sure."

Frank gives Olly's hair a quick ruffle and crouches next to him. Crinkling his forehead, he sighs and places a hand on his son's shoulder. "Whatever happens in life, Olly, I love you and will always have your back. You know that, right?"

"Sure, Dad." The second time he's been told that tonight, but the words deliver an unsettling feeling rather than intended reassurance.

"Okay, I best be off. I'll see you both later."

"Bye, Dad."

"I'll walk you out," Ivy says.

Olly inspects the rest of the contents of the box sitting on the kitchen table. There are pills of all different colours and sizes and enough bandages for some serious mummification. They'd recently learned about it at school, how the Egyptians used to wrap up their dead to stop the bodies rotting and smelling.

From the hallway, he hears his dad talking in hushed and urgent tones. He watches his nana's body language as she folds her arms and nods, finally giving her son a warm embrace. His dad opens the door, and Olly hears the rain pounding the street outside and feels the cold draught trespassing into the house. A flash of white illuminates the hallway and the faces on the paintings. *Nope, still scary.* Thunder rumbles almost instantaneously, setting off the first of many barking dogs from streets away.

"Bye, champ," his dad shouts.

The door closes, and Ivy rubs her hands together, making her way back down the hallway. "Vicious night. Can I get you a drink?"

"Okay, thanks. What do you have?"

"Soda, orange juice, beer."

He laughs, but her face remains unchanged. "Soda, please."

"Sit down at the table, love."

She gets two cans out of the cupboard. "Might be a bit flat—had it in for a while."

He wonders why old people buy soda if they have no intention of drinking it. And why the hell they didn't keep it in the fridge.

"Thanks." It is flat, warm too, but the sugar just about saves it.

"Now then, what do we have here?" she says, frowning and holding a palm out towards the pie.

"It's a cherry pie."

"Did your mum make it?"

Olly nods. "It's my absolute favourite."

"Tinned or fresh?" she asks?

"Huh?"

"The cherries. Tinned or fresh?"

He feels an inexplicable urge to lie, to get in his mum's corner. It doesn't make any sense, though, not after what she did.

"Tinned," he eventually mutters.

"Thought as much," she says, tutting loudly and shaking her head. She picks up the pie and flicks up the bin lid with a rather hefty stomp on the pedal.

"No, Nana, please don't—"

The pie hits the bottom of the bin with a loud thud. Olly thinks he hears the pie dish crack.

"It's not right, Olly." She walks over to the counter, pulls open the third drawer, and brings out a bright red oven mitt. Slipping her hand in the glove, she walks over to the oven and opens the door. Olly watches her pull out the first of many amazing looking pies. "Your dad told me cherry pie was your favourite."

The crust is golden and evenly so. To Olly, it resembles a small, deserted island and prompts a feeling of warmth across his skin. The lattice pastry provides a glimpse of the abundance of fruit underneath, and he hates to admit it, but the cherries look alive with flavour.

"It just doesn't make sense to me. Why go to all that trouble and not use fresh cherries? It really gets my goat."

She carefully places the pie on the cooling tray. "You might as well buy it from the store—some cheap Aunt Betty Boo mass-produced garbage. It doesn't make any sense, Olly. I tell you; it really gets my goat!"

She's turning a funny shade of red and beginning to breathe quite loudly. One of the lesions on her face is starting to leak a substance he assumes to be blood, but it's—*too dark?* He's still got a scab on his right knee from when he fell off his bike last week, and he can't help but pick it. His blood is, well, the colour of blood, and in the right light, even has a pinkish hue to it.

"If you are going to do a job, you do it properly. You don't take short cuts! It really gets my goat."

All he can do is stare, quietly watching her face turning an even darker shade. Part of him wants to ask about the goat. Perhaps later.

"You need to put the work in to get the rewards, Olly. It's like marriage. You've got to work at it and not give up when it gets difficult. You can't expect to produce a wonderful pie by doing things half-ass." She's spitting words out so fast that it sounds to Olly they will soon get caught in a big old pile up. "It gets my goat!"

As she pulls the large-bladed knife from the top drawer, he watches another lesion open up and begin to seep down her right cheek. She walks across to the pie and glances over his shoulder towards him. Olly nervously observes the blade trembling in her hand. From the corner of her mouth, a long string of saliva extends towards the ground. Her breasts are heaving as she gasps for breath.

"IT GETS MY FUCKING GOAT!"

She raises the knife high, maintaining eye contact, and brings the blade down hard into the centre of the pie. Olly recoils in the chair, suddenly feeling quite light-headed. He's never seen his nana like this before, and there's an overwhelming pang to be back home, surrounded by familiarity and predictable tension.

Still stooped over the pie, Ivy begins to cry. He follows the trail of a tear down her right cheek as it runs across the open sore and comes to a stop on her chin, threatening to fall into the pie below.

Not the pie. Not the pie.

It's as though time slows as he watches the droplet plummet towards the centre of the fruit and disappear into its darkness. He feels quite teary, as though he's had to endure an ordeal for nothing, like dying before reaching a save point in a game.

She staggers across to the table, pulls up a chair, and plants herself down. "I'm so sorry, love," she says, urgently reaching for his hands. "Oh, pet. I'm truly sorry. I'm in a lot of pain, you see. And I hate to see my little Frank upset. He puts on a brave face, but a mother can see. A mother has a sixth sense."

"It's okay, Nana." *You bloody loon.*

"No, it's inexcusable, Olly. I can't apologise enough. You'll learn one day, though—family is everything and that you'll protect them with everything you have. I know we don't see each other as often as I would like, and I guess you have your own life and friends and whatnot, but rest assured, I love you and Frank more than anything in the world."

She looks him in the eye. He wants to turn away but holds his gaze. His mum always tells him maintaining eye contact is an important sign of maturity.

"I promise that I will do everything in my power to protect you," she says, face taut with seriousness.

"Okay," is all he can muster.

"Let's make a fresh start," she adds, removing her hands and slapping them across her chunky thighs. "Now, what do you say to a big ole slice of Nana's cherry pie?"

His eyes are drawn to the glistening opening on her face that looks even worse now that she has wiped the tears away. It's as though someone has grabbed a handful of the warm fruit and shoved it in her face.

"Perhaps later, Nana."

"Okay, sure. Anyhow, we've got a couple of hours to kill before the doors open. What do you want to do? Game of cards, jigsaw?" She leans in close, and he can't help but stare at the seemingly endless chasm between her breasts. It's terrifying, but at the same time, he's feeling drawn towards it against his own free will.

"TV?" he says enthusiastically, moving his glance away.

"Ah, I don't really like having the television running, Olly. Lots of nonsense if you ask me."

So that's soda you buy and don't drink, and a TV in your lounge that you don't watch.

"What do you like to do, Nana?"

"Well, you've seen my paintings. That's a real passion for me. But I like gardening, too—you know—pottering around. I do a bit of knitting some-times when the mood takes me."

A mixture of boredom and uneasiness is already washing over Olly. He's only been there a few minutes, and she's already stabbed a pie, and now they're talking about gardening and knitting. He'd much rather be playing with his friends online or catching up on his favourite television show. He doesn't know where to look anymore. The choice is boobs or hanging jowls.

Her face is a hideous canvas of moles and bleeding sores clogged with excess make-up.

"What do you grow? In the garden."

"Well, that's for me to know and for you to find out, sonny."

He doesn't know what the means and doesn't really care.

"What's it like at home?" she asks. "You know, between your mum and dad."

Olly doesn't want to talk about it. The day is so far one of the worst he's had for a long time, and it's still very early.

"It's okay, I guess."

"You don't need to worry, okay? Someone your age shouldn't be anxious about stuff like this."

"I guess."

"As I said before, marriage is a journey and can be a lot of hard work. There's a quote. How does it go? Something along the lines of marriage being like war—long periods of boredom followed by short outbursts of conflict. But it's a partnership—it takes two people rowing in the same direction to get to where you need to be going. Take it from me—it certainly isn't easy."

"I just want everything to be okay," Olly says, a lump forming in his throat. He bites his lip to stem the sudden urge to cry.

"It will, Olly. I'm making a promise to you that it will."

Olly nods.

"Okay, you win. I'll stick the goggle box on for a bit, and you can show me what the kids are watching these days."

"Thanks, Nana."

The living room is warmer and cosier, and an old-looking electric fire has two of the three bars lit up. Across the arm of an old chair are a dozen or so knitting patterns and a well-used book of Sudoku puzzles. The couch has a half-finished scarf across the centre seat with two giant knitting needles emerging from the wool. More weird paintings furnish the wall, even stranger than the ones in the hallway. It's the stretched canvas made up entirely of fine red and yellow paints that grabs Olly's attention, though. From what he can see, it seems to be showing the aging process of the naked body, from infant to old age. The latter part of the picture consists of harder brushstrokes, thicker and deeper reds, unlike the paler light strokes on the left-hand side.

"It's one of my favourite paintings. I used old photographs of myself and blended them into a little montage, or as I call it, my little 'mont age'—clever, huh?"

He blushes and looks away. She notices his discomfort and offers a little laugh. "It's just art, Olly. I wanted to paint something that captured more than just a single moment in time. Anyone can do that with a camera, but I wanted to capture a lifetime."

Olly nods, still looking at the orange swirls in the brown carpet.

"Do you like painting, Olly?"

"It's alright, I guess."

"Next time, perhaps we can paint together."

"Can we watch TV now, please?"

"Sure, stick it on."

IVY WATCHES the boy turn the television on, and as he runs back towards the sofa, launching himself into the right-hand corner. She tries to remember what it felt like to move so freely, without pain, without fear of toppling, and with joints like springs. She watches him laugh and smirk at the banalest of things, shifting position frequently and changing the channel just as much, seemingly in an endless pursuit of something better than the programme before.

She loves the boy, though. She'll do everything to protect him.

CLEMENTINE

WATCHING the candle flicker violently in the draught from the bathroom window, Clementine enjoys the contrast of hot and cold as she immerses her prickling skin back into the warmth of the water. Turning the tap with her right foot, she rests her head on the back of the bubble-filled bath and focusses on the flow of water, trying not to think about anything. It's the first time all day she hasn't been able to smell the staleness that has been following her around.

It isn't long before her mind begins to fill with darkness, and the empty feeling returns. She moves her gaze to the medicine cabinet, as she has done on so many occasions of late. Wrapping her hands around the steel bars on the side of the bath, she pulls herself up and carefully reaches for it, catching her reflection in the glass. Pausing momentarily, she stares at the mirror, the snow-white hair framing a face she can hardly stand the sight of anymore. She opens the right-side door and grabs the bottle of pills from the second shelf and the small mouthwash glass from the one beneath, filling it half-full of cold water from the basin tap. Easing herself back into the water, she places the glass on the edge of the bath and twists off the bottle cap, emptying a handful of oval-shaped tablets into her palm.

More tears break through, as do memories that seemed far too long ago even to be real. "This is no fucking life," she says. "I'm so sorry, Alf."

Her cries become sobs, and the textured swirls in the ceiling merge into a single large whirlpool that she wants to disappear into.

"I'm so sorry!"

She hurls the pills and the bottle at the bathroom mirror and frantically begins thrashing at the water with her arms and legs, shaking her head aggressively from side to side. Giving a final synchronised splash of her arms, she lets out an animalistic howl so loud it reverberates in her chest. The glass tumbler smashes against the far wall as she swipes it away with her left arm.

Adrenaline starts to drop, and she slumps back, a heaving mess and feeling more alone than she ever has before.

ALEX

THERE IS ONLY DARKNESS. A muffled cry emerges as he tries to scream.

What's going on?

He tries to get up, but something is stopping him.

His head pounds, a dull but relentless and monotonous thud, and there's a more permanent pain running down his side. *Fuck. Fuck. Fuck.* He instinctively wants to cry, but that isn't going to help. He blinks his eyes profusely, hoping the glaze clears. *What is this thing? A wheelchair.* His hands and legs are bound by something, and with all his strength, he tries to wrestle free, but there's hardly any give.

Voices.

He tries to scream again, but only a smothered rasp emerges, followed by a stream of hot liquid from his nose. His vision is still drifting in and out of focus, but he can make out shelves. They're filled with what looks like cleaning products, large steel buckets, cloths. Momentarily, he thinks someone is standing in the corner of the room, and his stomach gives a nervous flutter, but it's only a mop resting against the wall.

The last thing he can remember was eating the pie. And the rain. He was running to get out of the rain.

He wonders what time it is. They were supposed to be having chips for tea.

What's that smell?

It's no good. He can't override the tears, and they come all at once and quickly. It's a short burst, but enough to make his face feel raw.

He begins to rock back and forth and side to side, picturing his mum stood at the bay window.

COMMUNITY CENTRE

As ANOTHER CRACK of thunder rings out across Newhaven Crescent, Ivy throws open the community centre doors, dragging Olly close behind. She puts the rain-drenched umbrella on the stand in the corner and gives out a big sigh of relief. The room is bigger than Olly expected, and already there's a decent level of chatter and activity as people line the bar and gossip about whatever old people gossip about.

Olly does a sweep of the room, observing the ones already sitting around the tables, tapping their feet, and strumming their bony fingers on the knees of their pants to music that sounds to him like it's breaking. The strong smell of beer does its best to mask the pungency of the old, but there's still a faint smell of urine and stale farts. *Not even a bloody fruit machine.* When things were better between his mum and dad, they used to go out for the occasional pub lunch on a Sunday, and his dad always let him have a shandy with his scampi and chips. He missed those days.

"So, who do we have here?" the stranger asks.

Ivy grabs him by the shoulders and thrusts him forward like a rugby prop. "Judith, this is Olly. Olly, this is Judith."

"Well, aren't you a handsome devil, Olly?"

He wants to retreat, back towards the relative safety of his nana, but doesn't want to offend the lady. Black spots the size of currants cover Judith's face, making her look a bit like an over-cooked fruit loaf. The smile she pulls causes them to crack, releasing small puffs of black dust in the air. He returns the smile, trying not to breathe them in.

"Oh, he's a picture," Edith shouts from the bar. She's wearing a gold paper crown, and a long green piece of glitter is draped over the shoulder of her blue dress. "Are you my birthday present, boy?"

"Take no notice of her," Judith says, taking his hand and leading him towards the bar. "Right, love. What can I get you to drink?"

"Shandy?" he asks, hopefully. Judith breaks into a smile.

"Oh, we've got a hardened drinker here!" she shouts. "Do you want a whisky chaser with that and a cigar?"

"No thanks."

"Hey, Trevor, can I get a pint of shandy for Lord Olly here? Easy on the lemonade. And I'll have two whisky and cokes, please, petal."

"Sure, Judith. Hey mate, are you ready for a good old-fashioned knees-up? Bet you think old people are boring, eh? Crosswords and Songs of Praise?"

Olly doesn't know what to say. "I guess so," he replies.

The music is deafening, but he's intrigued by the gramophone sitting on the bar. He remembers seeing one on an antique show that his mum likes to watch, but he's never seen one for real. The spin of the record is almost hypnotic, and the crackling music emerging from the ice-cream cone shape thing is quite haunting, as though within its darkness, there's a series of dark basements or alleys the sound is made to travel through first.

"Fascinating, isn't it?" Trevor shouts as he pulls a pint.

"Yes." And he means it. He plays music all the time through his phone and iPad, but this is something else. He doesn't understand all the lyrics to the one that is crackling through, but the music itself is making him feel quite sad.

"This one's been reconditioned to play more modern stuff. Fancy something with a bit more punch?" Trevor asks him. "I've got some awesome stuff under the counter."

Olly nods and watches as Trevor lifts the small arm away that houses the needle. From beneath the bar, he pulls out a box full of dog-eared record sleeves and begins to sift through them.

"My dad has got a record player, but it looks nothing like this," Olly shouts. This one is so cool!"

"I know. Sometimes we swap vinyls. He's got one of my Pink Floyd's at the moment."

"You know my dad?"

"For sure," he replies. "Hey, this will get your feet tapping. Sweet Caroline —Neil Diamond."

There are cheers as the track kicks in, and as Trevor promised, Olly begins tapping his feet. Although quite dizzy with the busyness of the place and the dialogue, he's pleasantly surprised by how much he's enjoying the attention and atmosphere. He feels quite grown up and not shy like with adults of his mum and dad's age.

"It's Olly, isn't it?" The old man thrusts his little hand out and breaks into a game show host smile that exposes over-sized dentures. He's dressed head to toe in blue suede with sequin-encrusted lapels the size of dinner plates. His eyes are wide with excitement, and the caverns that run across his forehead indicate a well-lived life. There's a tuft of rusty hair sprouting from his forehead.

Olly shakes the man's hand and nods.

"I'm Rodney. Pleasure to meet you, champ."

Olly struggles to tear his gaze away from the enormous gnashers. "And you."

"We are going to have so much fun tonight—I tell ya!"

Olly smiles. "I don't really know what is happening, but if you say so."

"Trust me, son, you're in for a treat. We're going to bring this house down."

"Cool."

"What sports are you into, kid?"

"None really. I play a bit of soccer now and again."

"Ah, yeah. I had trials for Bristol once. Who do you support?"

"Liverpool," Olly volunteers, hoping it's the end of the conversation. He's watched them play one game in three years, and can't even remember the name of the stadium, never mind the name of any players on the team.

"Cool bananas. By the way, what shall I put you down for tonight?"

"Eh?"

"For talent night. What are you going to do for us tonight? You have to do something, everyone is—doesn't matter what," Rodney insists, rubbing his hands firmly together.

"I don't know."

"Come on, don't be shy. Everybody's got one."

"Arm farts. I can do arm farts!"

"Christ, I'm not sure if this place can handle any more farts, but I'll put you down."

"Rodney!" someone shouts from the back.

"Have to crack on, champ. We've got a big one lined up tonight!"

"Here you go, love," Judith says. "Let's go and grab our table."

"Thanks!" Olly follows Judith to where Janet is already seated, her plump arms taking up nearly half the table.

"You must be Olly," Janet says. "Sit." She kicks a chair towards him.

"Thanks."

"Edith will be joining us, too. By the way, I think she's got her eye on you, so watch out."

"Okay."

"Here's your drink, Janet," Judith says, sliding it across into Janet's waiting hand. The move is impressive, and Olly guesses it's not the first time they've done it.

His eyes fall across the small stack of books in the centre of the table; they're bright red with something he doesn't recognise written down the spine. He thinks about reaching for one but feels a hand coil around his right shoulder blade and instinctively turns to see a giant in a thin black suit wearing a gas mask. Olly's heart pounds, and he recoils slightly. There's no respite as the strange man begins to breathe heavily through the mask.

"Don't let Benji scare you," Janet utters. "He's harmless. Ugly as sin, but harmless."

The man provides a final and sinister sigh before making his way to the bar.

"Is that why he wears the mask?" Olly whispers.

"That, and the fact he can't stand the smell of old people, himself included."

Olly watches as Benjamin walks over to the bar, fascinated with how he intends to drink anything. Trevor puts a glass full of dark brown liquid down, and Olly observes the tall and lanky man bending over, nursing an extended black straw from the mask into the drink. Like a fly, Olly thinks.

It strikes him that he hasn't seen his nana since she introduced him to Judith. He scans the tables and the bar, but there's no sign of her anywhere.

"She'll be around the back, preparing, Olly. Don't worry," Judith consoles, noting his concern. She gives him a pat on the shoulder.

"Preparing for what?"

"For the talent show, silly," she replies with a wink.

"Edith, come on!" Janet shouts. "We're starting."

There's a hush around the room. Someone farts, but nobody draws attention to it.

"Testing. Testing. Can all you old buggers hear me okay?"

There are a few "ayes" from around the room. "I can't hear a bloody thing," someone shouts from table two. Olly peers around Janet's big head to see.

"Have you got your hearing aid turned on, Barney?"

"Eh?"

"Hearing aid!" Rodney shouts.

"My spade?"

"Lucy, make sure the silly fucker has his hearing aid turned on, will you?"

Janet turns to Olly and raises her eyebrows. He giggles and shakes his head.

Grabbing the chair opposite Olly, Edith sits down with a sigh. She gives his foot a gentle nudge with hers and blows a kiss.

"He's good to go," Lucy shouts.

"Good evening, old and young. First of all, thanks for your attendance tonight. It's going to be an absolute cracker."

There are a few piercing wolf whistles from the crowd, but Janet takes the biscuit with an ear-splitter. It's still ringing in Olly's ears as Rodney the Smurf, which Olly has decided to name him, continues the welcome address.

"Can we all give a warm welcome to our young guest, Olly Rogers! Raise your glasses, people."

There are loud cheers and a few drum rolls on tables. Olly can feel his cheeks turning red, but he isn't averse to the attention. He raises his pint glass in the air and stands to perform a small bow to further applause and whistles.

"Now, I'll get this out the way quickly as I am as keen to get on with the festivities as anyone, but I feel this needs to be said. Can we please refrain from any fistfights this week? There are thirty-four people in this room with weak bladders, and we have one shared toilet. I ask that you queue in an orderly fashion and give each other the necessary respect. Can I get a yeah on this motion, please?"

There are murmurs of agreement from the audience.

"Good. Okay then, it's tiiiiiiiiiiiiiiiiime!"

The blue Smurf in his element now, strutting up and down the stage like a rock star.

"Please welcome our first act to the stage. Benjamin, come on down!"

There's a generous amount of clapping and cheering as the man in the mask makes his way to the front.

Olly looks around the room, searching for his nana, but still can't see her. He does catch sight of a woman with white hair whipped up like candy floss staring back at him. She's wearing a bright green cocktail dress, but her face is contrastingly pale, and she looks quite sad. He smiles, unsure if she will notice. She turns away, focussing on Benjamin, who is whispering something into Rodney's ear.

"Sorry, all. I meant to say, please welcome Darth Vader to the stage."

"Get on with it," someone from the front table shouts.

There is a loud inhale, followed by an exhale. "How did I know what Luke was getting for his birthday?"

"Who's Luke?" the woman in the leather jacket with a ring through her lip shouts from the table next door.

Benjamin breathes in and out once more. "From Star Wars, you ignoramus."

"Never seen it," she shouts back.

"I don't know, Darth Vader," Rodney interjects. "How did you know what Luke was getting for his birthday?"

Benjamin gives another loud inhale and exhale.

"Come on, Benji, don't keep us in suspenders," Rodney prompts.

The mask fogs up again. "It's on the tip of my tongue."

"I don't get it," someone in the front shouts.

"Fuck's sake, let's give someone else a turn, shall we?" Rodney gives his smile, ushering Benjamin off stage.

"Wait, there's more," Benjamin protests, his breathing becoming quicker.

"Okay, next on the list tonight is—Norman. He says he's been practising this one for a few weeks but now has it down pat. A big round of applause, please. Come on, Norman!"

Darth Vader leaves the stage, shaking his head. He flicks his lengthy middle digit at one of the tables as he takes his place back at his own.

Norman is completely bald and has ears as big as trophy handles. He's wearing a tartan tank top and has both his hands shoved in oversized grey slacks. He moves his mouth close to the microphone and then back again, letting out a nervous cough. He tries again, but this time barks directly into the mike. "Excuse me, sorry." He coughs again, even louder, prompting people to cover their ears. And again, and again. He starts to hack rather violently, doubling over and retching at the floor.

"Are you going to cough up a hairball, Norman? Is that the act?" someone shouts from the right.

But he carries on, relentlessly heaving at the ground.

"I hope Rodney's saved the best acts 'til last. This is abysmal," Judith says to the table.

Norman crouches to the ground. He has his hands to his neck and looks to be in agony. Olly stands up, seemingly the only one with concern for the poor man. The hack turns to a dry rasp, as though he has something stuck in his throat.

The women at his table are obliviously chatting about the lady with candy floss hair. He hears one of them say, "losing the plot," but the rest of the conversation is distant. Norman is squirming on stage, legs jerking erratically.

"Breakdancing's no longer a thing, Norm," someone else shouts, inducing raucous laughter and clinking glasses.

"Try spinning on your ear, Norm," someone else adds. "I bet you'd never stop."

"It's alright, young Olly; this happens sometimes," Judith reassures.

The man stops moving and starts to emit a desperate choking sound. His eyes are bulging, just like a frog's. Olly looks around to see if anyone is phoning for an ambulance, but everyone is seated and laughing or chatting as though this is Rodney's usual routine. *Christ, there's something—his mouth!* He watches Norman release a huge bark, projecting something onto the stage floor with a soft thud. Standing on his tiptoes, Olly cranes his neck to get a better view. He can't see too clearly, but it looks like a fat worm, glistening under the bright white of the spotlight.

"Can we get a dustpan and brush, please, Doris? And will someone pass Norman his beer?"

The novelty of being surrounded by elders is beginning to wear off for Olly. He watches Norman being helped off stage and back to his table. X-factor, this isn't. If he could see his nana, he would tell her that he wanted to go home now.

"Where's Ivy?" he says to Edith.

"Don't worry, pet; she'll be here soon. Relax. Do you want to come and sit on Edith's knee?"

"I'm fine, thanks."

He pats the pocket of his jeans, taking some comfort in the hard casing of his mobile phone. The last thing he'd want to do is interrupt his parents as they tried to work things out, but he would if he had to.

"Well, I don't think any of us expected that," Rodney chirps. "Ten out of ten for effort, though!"

"I need another drink," Edith says. "My round kidder. I'll get you a cider. Same again for you girls?"

"Line 'em up," Judith replies. "We're gonna need them by the looks of it."

Olly remembers having a sip of his mum's cider once. He liked it. On any other occasion, he would be excited about the prospect, but something is unsettling him, aside from the crazies and the escalating odour of fart gas. What did Nana call it? A sick sense. He pats the pocket of his pants once more, not sure how long he'll be able to resist the temptation.

"Next on stage, Albert! This evening, Albert is going to be performing a magic trick, so keep your eyes peeled. Doris, can we have a chair on stage for this one, please?"

There's a murmur of excitement from the crowd as the man in the track-suit takes to the stage, waiting for poor Doris to drag the chair across for him. Finally, Albert eases himself down, and the crowd falls silent. He's a funny-looking man, all beard and ear hair.

"Judith," Olly whispers.

"Shh." She waves a hand at him.

"Janet," Olly mutters, but nothing.

Olly turns towards Edith as the last hope. "Where's the loo, Edith?"

"Wait until Houdini's finished, and I'll take you. Even help you get it out if you want."

There's a low moan coming from the stage, and Olly turns his attention back to Albert to see the man gripping the seat of the chair and shaking profusely. He's going quite red.

"He's having a stroke," someone calls out.

"Shh," the crowd hisses in unison.

Oddly, Olly finds himself thinking about Nana's kettle, the way it shakes so vigorously the closer it gets to boiling. He half expects steam to begin emerging from the old man's fuzzy ears.

Rodney's face is also a picture of concern as he marches back on stage, nervously smiling, trying to make eye contact with Albert. The old man dismisses him with a wave.

"I really need the loo," Olly says to anyone that's listening.

Albert's face is the same shade as his nana's from earlier now, but he's not finished yet. Even from so far back, Olly can see the veins popping in the old man's neck. Something is leaking onto his shirt and spreading fast.

"What is he doing?" Janet comments.

Albert's face is red raw and looks like it might ignite at any moment. Olly wouldn't be that surprised if it did, based on already seeing a man regurgitate something the size of a large sausage from his mouth. The groan is escalating, and the shaking is settling. His face is the colour of beetroot. Something is going to happen.

There are gasps from the crowd as something noisily clatters to the floor. Olly isn't sure what is happening at first, but he catches sight of something rolling jerkily across the wooden boards, eventually coming to rest in one of the cracks.

The crowd begins to clap. "Seen it all now," Janet spits before knocking back her drink.

"Come on then, young man. Let's go and choke that rooster of yours."

"Eh?"

"Toilet, love."

He follows her as she weaves between the tables towards the front of the room. "Bring him back in one piece," someone shouts from the left. "Bit old for you, isn't he?" someone else says from the right. There's a sudden sting on his right buttock, and he turns to see a burly woman wearing a strange cat mask that covers half of her face. She blows him a kiss and offers a little wave.

"Okay, it's second on your left down the corridor. If you need me, shout."

"Can someone give Albert his eye back, please," Rodney pleads. "Now come on, stop tossing it around. If it goes down the vent, we'll never get it back."

It's a dimly lit hallway, occasionally falling into darkness as the flickering tube above sizzles. There are two doors to the left, one at the far end of the corridor and another to the right.

The door to the first room is ajar, and there's a lady with a perm sat on a small bench wearing a fairy dress. She's grimacing and groaning as she struggles to get her feet into a small pair of ballet shoes. There's a stream of dark blood dripping from between her legs that immediately makes Olly feel quite wobbly. She glances at him as he walks past, and Olly offers a fake smile, but she swings the door shut, grunting something inaudible. He moves his hand to his front pocket.

"Let's welcome on stage, Micky the Mime!"

Some relief kicks in as he eyes the sign for the toilet, but a sharp noise to his right grabs his attention—*Storeroom.* He glances behind to find Edith absorbed with the current act on stage—some guy prancing around with big red lips and a white powdery face.

There it is again. He's busting now but needs to find out what is making the sounds. Checking over his shoulder, he whispers, "Hello," hoping for no reply. Nothing. Just more clanging. He reaches for the handle, heart pounding and nerve endings tingling. He counts to three and begins to turn it, slowly and already with some regret. Handle fully down, he gives the door a nudge, but it doesn't move—*locked.*

"Kid!"

Sharply inhaling, Olly turns to see a stocky old man wearing a bobble hat, buckling up his belt. "Toilet's free, if that's what you're looking for, kiddo."

"Yes, thanks," Olly mutters.

"Rats!" the man says on the way past. There's a dark stain spreading down the man's right leg.

"Huh?"

"In the storeroom. We've put some poison down. They'll be dead rats before long."

Olly nods.

As soon as Olly steps foot in the toilet, he begins to gag, not a dry retch like before. Vomit, the colour of orangeade projects from his mouth onto the floor. He reaches out to the wall for stability, and he feels his hand sinking into stickiness. There are huge blobs of foul darkness scattered across all four walls, but it's the display in the toilet bowl that Olly struggles with the most. It's a bubbling mess of foulness. He tries to flush it away, but it refuses to move, as though it's a living organism doing everything it can to survive. He watches it pulsate, a six-headed shit monster that he half expects to start crawling up the bowl.

Christ on a bike.

Urgently, Olly unzips and takes two steps back. He aims, he fires, he misses, but he no longer cares; he just wants to get out. There is undeniable relief as the pressure eases from his bladder. He pushes out the remaining dribble with a groan.

Perhaps they've sorted it out by now. They've had some time.

As Olly reaches for his phone, the door rattles.

"Are you in there, Olly?" Edith's voice. "Come on; you're missing all the acts."

He holds his breath and holds the phone in the air.

"Olly!"

"Just a minute," he replies, adjusting the angle and height of the phone to try and get some bars.

"Viola's doing the Nutcracker."

He stands on the bowl, but it's no good, no bars. "I'm having a poo," he yells. A key begins to rattle in the door, and he jumps down.

"What's going on in here?" she asks. "Why are your hands behind your back?"

"I want to go home," he says.

"Nonsense, the night's just getting started. Is that a phone?"

"Yes."

"Oh, Olly, you won't get a signal down here, love."

"Why?"

"What the heck have you done in there?" she asks, arching her neck to survey the damage.

"It wasn't me. It was the guy with the hat," he says, frantically washing his hands in the small basin.

The scratchy music begins once more as Edith begins hustling him back through the room. Viola is really going for it, and Olly can't tell if the cracks are from the music or the old lady's bones rubbing together. She spins, she tries to jump, she leans with arm stretched out and almost topples, but she appears to be enjoying every minute of it.

Judith looks back at him and smiles. "How's your night, kidder?"

"Okay, but I'd like to go home now."

He's not sure if she hears him above the music, but she turns back to the act.

"Good. Drink your cider, love," she says. "Plenty more where that came from."

Viola finishes the act to tremendous applause and whistles. The flowers from some of the vases are tossed onto the stage, and even a giant pair of underpants find their way to the floor. She takes another bow.

"Alright, time's up, sweetheart," Edith comments. "Now fuck off."

The clapping begins to die down a little, but Viola is still enjoying being on stage. She flashes her smile, does another little spin, and takes yet another bow.

"Jesus," Judith hisses.

"Is he up next?" Janet says, and they both laugh.

As if Rodney can sense the looming heckles, he rushes on stage and gently guides Viola away from the centre. "Fantastic. By the way, everyone, the local ballet school charity football match was an absolute cracker. It ended up two-two."

The joke goes over Olly's head, but he didn't miss much, judging by the moans. The funny lady with white hair is staring at him again. She offers a smile this time, and he returns it.

"Next up is Geoff," Rodney says, reading from his card. "Geoff is going to perform Ennio Morricone's theme for 'The Good, The Bad and The Ugly' using his box of toenails."

"Sweet Jesus," Olly whispers under his breath. It's one of his dad's favourite expressions. He takes a mouthful of cider and enjoys the sweetness it brings.

Damn it!

His stomach gives a little flutter as he contemplates his behaviour towards his mum over the last few days. He's so torn—it's not fair. He knows she hasn't been happy of late, but if she just tried that little bit harder, as Nana said, then it might work out. When he found the half-naked photo of Roger, he felt more hurt than angry, but it's changed over time. He doesn't know what to think, but there's one thing for sure—he hates that prick, Roger.

The piercing whistling sound that Geoff delivers prompts more than half the room to cover their ears. It's a slow and weird tune that Olly has never heard before. Every so often, Geoff holds the box close to the microphone and gives it a little shuffle, followed by more grating whistling. He looks so proud of himself, ignoring the boos coming from the floor. To Olly, the slowness of the tune makes it feel like it's never going to end, and there is nothing else for him to do but take another mouthful of that oh-so-sweet cider.

Finally, Geoff takes a bow to a smattering of applause and is quickly ushered off by Rodney.

"What a variety of acts so far, ladies and gentlemen. It makes you wonder what other treasures we'll be uncovering tonight."

There's a knock on the door of the community centre that prompts every head to turn. The music stops. In contrast to the previous rowdiness of the crowd and volume of the gramophone, Olly thinks he could hear a pin drop.

"Someone going to get that?" Rodney finally calls out, breathing loudly down the microphone.

Janet slides her chair away and walks over, unbolting the door and pulling it slightly ajar.

As Olly peers through the gap, a flash of white outlines the uniforms of the two police officers. A conversation ensues, but a long and ominous rumble of thunder prevents him from overhearing anything important. He keeps his eye on Janet, though, as she repeatedly shakes her head and shifts her glance between the young man and woman. Finally, she steps aside and ushers them in. As the officers shake themselves off, Janet marches down the side of the room to where Rodney is standing and whispers something in his ear. He nods, and with head bowed, walks back onto the stage, giving the microphone a quick double tap to make sure he has everyone's attention.

"Sorry, ladies and gents, just a quick break in proceedings. It might be nothing, and I certainly hope so, but a young boy has apparently gone missing. We all know him as our paperboy, Alex. His parents are very concerned as he would normally have been back over two hours ago. Has anyone seen him within that period?"

The room is a sea of shaking heads. Olly notices the female officer looking towards him, and he automatically feels nervous. The male officer is tapping his right foot and glancing around as if he has better things to do with his time.

Rodney sighs down the microphone once more. "Hopefully, he's just playing silly beggars or run away from home, probably hiding in the back garden somewhere. I will ask that if anyone does see or hear anything, you report it to the police immediately, as I don't know about you, but I certainly can't do without my Sunday papers." His voice crackles towards the end, most likely aware there's a time for jokes and a time not to be a total clown.

"What's your name, boy?" the female officer asks as she makes her way to the table.

"Olly," Edith answers for him.

Olly immediately feels the need to clam up, shuffling awkwardly in his chair. The officer glances towards the cider sitting in front of him, and Judith instinctively picks it up and knocks half of it back. She hasn't had cider in years, and the rip-roaring belch that immediately escapes her mouth reminds her why. On the side of his cheek, Olly feels the projected warmth and gets a whiff of something quite horrific mixed with the fruity goodness.

"You're a bit young for this place, aren't you, Olly?" the officer says, eyeing Judith warily.

"I'm—I'm here with my nana," he replies.

"That's nice. Olly, this boy that's gone missing is about your age. I don't suppose you know him, do you—Alex Taylor?"

He looks away and frowns. He's never heard of the kid, but he wants to let her know he's giving it some serious thought. "No, sorry."

"We'll be in touch if we hear anything," Janet adds.

"Same goes for everyone," the officer says, raising her voice. "We might need to come back and talk to you all later. Let's just hope he turns up."

"I'm sure he will," Judith volunteers.

"Okay, thanks for your time, and enjoy your night. Looks like a riot," the officer says, winking at Olly. "Come on, George."

Judith gets up and walks them back to the door, locking it quickly behind them. Trevor kicks off the music again, and the chatter resumes.

"Liz, you're up. Come on down!" Rodney says enthusiastically, looking to lift the tempo. "Gottle of Geer."

Olly watches the lady on the table opposite reach into an old-fashioned-looking suitcase. She's wearing glittery lipstick and ridiculously long fake eyelashes. Giddily, she makes her way to the stage, carrying what looks like a small doll wearing a chequered jacket and bow tie. She sits on the chair with the dummy on her lap, inhales deeply, and begins.

"You're ugly," the dummy says.

"Speak for yourself," she replies.

"I wish I could."

Olly looks across at the clock: 8:30. It feels so much later. He stares at the golden liquid in the glass and feels his eyes beginning to close. The voice on the stage begins to fade. It's usually well after nine that he begins to feel tired, but he's overcome with exhaustion and longs for the peacefulness of his room. *What if they can't work it out? What if we have to move to a new house? What if I have to choose?*

His head drops, but the explosion of laughter startles him, and he looks up to find Albert and Norman playing football with the dummy's head. Liz is still sat on stage in tears, cradling the headless dummy like a teddy bear.

"I always thought you'd give good head, Liz," someone shouts to raucous laughter.

As if sensing a possible loss of control, Rodney steps in quickly and gives the microphone another series of loud taps. "Harry, you're up. Put the ball, I mean head away lads, come on."

Liz walks off the stage solemnly and takes her place to a smattering of applause. Albert gives the head back to her, undamaged but with very dishevelled hair, offering an apology that doesn't appear to be accepted.

"Harry, come on. We've still got lots to get through."

"Coming," he replies, hobbling on stage.

"Ladies and Gents, may I present Harry and his moonwalking."

Olly immediately recognises the Michael Jackson song, and it delivers a twinge of sadness. When things were okay at home, he and his mum sometimes baked together on a Saturday morning. They would have a little dance-off, taking it in turns to make up the wildest dance possible. They would have each other in stitches. One time, they lost the plot and started throwing flour at each other until they collapsed in a heap of hysterics and began to make snow angels on the kitchen floor. Dad came home and said it looked like the murder scene of Santa Claus and one of his elves. He finds himself longing for that feeling of security once more.

Harry takes to the stage in a trilby and leather jacket. He's so tall and thin, and to Olly, from where he's sitting, the guy resembles a clothes hanger. Not letting go of his crotch for the entire act, Harry swings his hips this way and that, alternating between dramatic grunting noises and genuine moans of agony. He finishes the act with his signature move.

"Wow, thanks, Harry. You might need some muscle spray and painkillers after that. Right, who do we have next? Let me see—Olly! I've heard this act is the pits, but let's give him a big round of encouragement."

He forgot. *Oh shit.* All eyes turn towards him. "Olly, Olly, Olly!" Edith chants. The entire room begins to join in, banging on tables, whistling, and shouting words of encouragement.

Olly begins shaking his head at Janet, but she salutes and flicks her head towards the stage.

"Go on, boy," Judith prompts in her husky voice. "I'll get you another cider!"

The night seems dreamlike, like one of those out-of-body experiences he's read about. There's another flutter in his stomach, and he's not sure if it's the cider or a physical reaction to the bizarre events taking place in this alien world of fart gas and bad breath.

Gas mask man is staring directly at him, and it's not helping. The room suddenly feels so big.

"One quick one," Judith says. "For me."

To rapturous applause, he takes the first step away from the relative comfort of the chair and begins making his way towards the stage. He does his best to avoid the knobbly fingers reaching out towards him, quickly shuffling down the centre of the room. Leaping on stage, he takes position behind the microphone, unbuttoning his shirt and staring towards the floor at the circle of white that surrounds him. A wolf whistle emerges from the back of the room, and he knows even without looking that it's Edith. He slips his arm underneath his pit and slowly brings his elbow up. With blood pounding in his ears, he looks towards the hungry crowd and holds his position. Counting down from three, he finally snaps his arm down to produce the perfect raspberry that fills the entire room with desired grossness.

Silence.

Suddenly, the crowd goes nuts—a tidal wave of ear-splitting applause rushing from the back of the room to the front, and Olly can't stop the big cheesy smile from breaking across his face. He performs his masterpiece again, and it sends the crowd even crazier. And Again. Again. They all start copying, unbuttoning shirts and blouses and creating their own little symphony of farts. The entire room is at it, in stitches, egging each other on and slapping each other's backs with congratulatory praise. Olly feels magnificent, like a conductor leading his band through the world championships.

He senses more eyes on him, and he snaps his head to the left to see his nana looking at him from the door at the far end of the corridor. She closes it abruptly.

There are more acts, ranging from strange to strangely terrifying. Highlights being Joan's animal impressions, Cora's sword swallowing, and Jimmy's boomerang foot—so named because arthritis has moulded it over time to look like it was coming back in on itself.

"Okay, we only have two more acts left, my good friends. Please welcome the one and only—Clementine."

To thunderous clapping, the white-haired lady limps to the stage and is given a helping hand by Rodney as he pulls her over the step. "Clementine will be doing a little number you will all recognise, called "We'll Meet Again." Let's hear it once more for our very own diva."

Applause dwindles as the music begins, and Olly watches the white-haired lady with interest as she begins her short gingerly walk to the stage. As she makes it to the spotlight, though, she starts to ooze confidence, grabbing the microphone and carefully stepping over the lead to get into position.

"She's not been looking herself of late," Judith says to the table.

Janet nods. "She hasn't been right for a while."

The voice that floats across makes the hairs bristle on the back of Olly's neck. It's not his taste by any means, but he knows a good singer when he hears one and wishes his mum was here to enjoy it. There's a sadness about the lady on stage, one he noticed when he first caught her looking at him, the music making it even more perceptible. He scans the room to see people wiping tears away. Even Janet has smudged mascara, and Benjamin is working a hand under his mask. Back on stage, the spotlight shows off the glistening streak running down Clementine's face, and that makes Olly feel quite watery, too. Her voice holds all the way through, and it's only as she finishes that her voice quivers. "That song is dedicated to my late husband, Alf." She hands the microphone back to Rodney and walks off the stage to silence.

"Wow, that one pulled at the heartstrings. It's the worst when someone steals your heart like that. I always wonder if the culprit will get—wait for it—cardiac arrested. Bum bum!"

The silence continues.

"Okay, so we just need a few minutes to set up the next and final act of the show. Don't fear, though. Trevor and Doris will be bringing a little treat around for you shortly. Can I ask if there's anyone here that doesn't like cherries?"

Only Norman puts his hands up. "Blueberries okay, Norm?"

"Aye."

"This is my favourite bit," Edith comments. "You tried Ivy's pies before, Olly?"

"No."

"Oh, they're to die for, my friend," she says.

"Lights, Doris," Rodney says. "And Trevor, can we have the music, please?"

Darkness blankets them, and it takes a few seconds for that charcoal grey effect to provide at least some visibility for Olly. "What's going on?"

"It's alright, love. Must be something special happening on stage."

The room is lit up with a flash of white, and a crashing roll of thunder adds to the unease Olly already feels. There's some activity in the stage area, and he can hear a strange squeaking sound, but as he arches his neck and strains his eyes to see, he can only make out silhouettes.

A clatter takes him by surprise, and to his right, he finds a generous slice of pie in a dish, a scoop of ice-cream on the side. "Thanks," he says to Doris, who continues speed walking around the table. He hungrily picks up the spoon but has a flashback to Nana dripping into the fruit, and it all plays out in his head again in horrific slow-motion. There were at least three more pies in the oven, though, and a groan of his stomach prompts him to play the odds.

He picks up the spoon and cracks through the crust, watching the fruit bleed into the snowball of ice-cream. Nana was right, the taste is something else, and the fresh cherries take it to a different league. He savours every mouthful and all the contrasting textures and layers that swirl towards his throat. The wholesomeness of the experience alleviates some of his nervousness and out of place anxiety, and as he takes his last mouthful, he sits back in the chair feeling much more relaxed. Staring at the ceiling, he feels pleasantly dizzy, and the darkness begins to wrap around him and draw him in. It feels like he's floating, weightless as he reaches towards it, as though he's spacewalking like he's seen on TV, but without the tether of a rope. The renewed chatter of the crowd is fading, and the sound of cutlery against the bowl seems distant and drawn out, as though time is being slowed down. It's just him and the music as he glides further into the void, shedding his fears and anxious thoughts. There is some light at the end of the darkness now. His ascent is getting faster, as though the light is pulling him towards it, hurtling him at ever-increasing speed through the makeshift tunnel. He can see a door, and—*Nana?*

There's a voice, slow and distant. "Olly."

He's getting closer now, and the increasing white light is making him squint. It is her; it's Nana. Breakneck speed now, the door approaches, but just as he is about to let himself bask in the offered warmth of the light, she closes the door, and he is left aimlessly spinning in the darkness again. He feels something on his shoulder and turns to see a long and spindly alien-like tentacle coiling around his shoulder.

"Olly." The voice is clearer, closer. He begins to fall backwards, descending with speed towards the sounds of chatter and footsteps that have resurrected. Suddenly, he is back in his chair, Edith's fingers gently squeezing. "Olly, are you with us?"

"Yes," he replies, but his voice seems odd, deeper somehow. It causes him to let out a giggle.

"Good pie isn't it?" she says.

"The best," Olly replies to the lady that currently has two mouths and three eyes. There's another flash of lightning, and the static frame develops in Olly's mind of Rodney on stage, watching Doris pushing something along. *A wheelchair?*

"Olly, attention on the stage now, please. Guess who's next?" Edith says.

"Lights, please!" Rodney calls out. There's a pitter-patter of footsteps, and the room lights up once again, causing Olly's vision to swim with pulsating shadowy floaters. He squelches at his eyes, but it fails to displace them. The floaters begin to merge into even larger beating organisms until the lava lamp blobs finally combine to create a single misty film. There is something sitting in the chair, moving, squirming—his blurry vision only feeding back what looks like a giant white worm.

The mistiness is coming and going, things swimming in and out—faces and objects. What sounds like an explosion outside vibrates the floor and rides through him from foot to head. He looks around the room, and all he can see are inane grins baring teeth like cityscapes. Benjamin looks across at him and waves. *Darth Vader just waved at me.* He starts to giggle, which turns into a laugh, which turns into complete hysterics. Struggling to get air in, he is lost, unable to find a way back to self-control. His insides are sore from laughing so much, and he wills himself to stop. Finally, after a few stop-starts, he begins to bring himself back.

"Our final act tonight, ladies and gents, is the wonderful Edith Marone. Happy Birthday, Edith!"

The music kicks in—an exotic slow beat that reminds Olly of a chocolate advert. Edith is nearly at the stage, but before she takes the step up, she wraps her green glitter around Albert's neck, hikes up her dress, and sits in his lap. Olly watches her whisper something in the old man's ear and run her fingers through his beard, which causes Albert's skin to turn lobster red. There's laughter and jeering throughout. Someone even shouts, "You'll have his eye out with those!"

Olly's head is spinning, a montage of sounds and imagery. The white thing in the wheelchair continues to worm around. He screws his eyes semi-closed to try and block everything out, focussing his attention on what's in the chair. There are two eye holes cut out near the top. *Holy Shit! It's a—person.*

Edith leaves Albert's lap and makes her way to the stage, trailing the glitter behind her and walking in a way that makes her look like she's on a tightrope. It's the occupant of the wheelchair's turn to bear Edith's weight as she straddles across the chair, draping the green glitter around the mystery guest. She leans back and works one of her heels loose. Olly watches its flight path as she flings it over her head and into the crowd. Harry is quick to his feet, catching it in his left hand at full stretch. Bringing the shoe to his nose, he inhales deeply, and seemingly satisfied, takes his seat once again. She tosses the next one into the audience, but Olly loses sight of it among the crowd of hopefuls.

From what feels like so far away, Judith is talking to Janet about the invasion of black mole-like blemishes and how much she cannot wait to be rid of them. Janet lifts her neck to expose the giant black worm that seems to be a full-time resident of her throat.

Edith is unpeeling her stockings as the person beneath her continues to thrash away. She swings them above her head like a lasso and launches them at the closest table. Spilling from the lap of the wheelchair occupant, she stands and turns away from the crowd, giving a little bum jiggle and starting work on the zipper at the back of her dress.

For Olly, the room continues to spin in kaleidoscopic patterns, throwing images that unhinge and disorientate: sea worms caught in black fish nets, the dummy head choking up a black glob of matter, false teeth chasing him down the corridor and leading him back to the six-headed shit monster. He puts his head in his hands and tries to focus his attention on the conversation of the two women at his table, paying attention to every word, every syllable, in the hope it might help ground him.

"Really? Judith remarks. "That's just awful. Sometimes when I wake, there's just a pile of black goo in the bed. It smells so foul."

"I can't wait for tonight," Janet says. "I might appear as hard as nails, but it gets to me. Better than the alternative, though, I suppose."

"Shit, yeah," Judith agrees. "Whatever it takes."

He glances back to the stage to see Edith's lacy bra, the dress now around her waist. She catches his eye and blows him a kiss, prompting him to turn away quickly to study the rusty wheel of the table leg that acknowledges him with a wink. He looks back at the ceiling, hoping it will pull him back in and rip him away from the chaos happening on stage, but the rectangular tiles begin to pull away, disappearing into a vortex of dirty yellow light.

"And the rest," he hears someone shout.

"Harry, put it away, you dirty old sod!" someone from the table hollers.

He looks towards the bar and sees the horn of the gramophone mouthing something at him. "I can't hear you," Olly shouts. The opening gets bigger, but he still can't understand what it's saying.

Is this what it feels like to be drunk? I only had a shandy and half a pint of cider.

"I'm sorry. I still can't hear you!" Olly shouts.

The mouth of the gramophone continues to expand, chewing inaudible words out. As Olly turns his head and leans in towards it, he's plucked from the chair and sent on a disorienting loop-the-loop around the inside of the horn. Finally, he pops out the end, feeling his stomach flip as he freefalls onto the ringed black surface of the vinyl record. Round and round he goes, ducking each time the arm of the gramophone threatens to take him out. The rotations are getting faster each time, forcing him to crouch, but the dizzying acceleration continues to disorient and blur his vision. Finally, it all gets too much, and he sprawls himself across the blackness. He watches the tables flashing by with dizzying speed until he is launched headfirst towards the other side of the room. He's floating a few inches below the ceiling, looking down on the folk of Newhaven Crescent. On stage, Edith is now without her dress. Only the lacy bra and huge panties keep her naughty bits from being on display. The writhing body continues its struggle but appears to be growing weary, its movements less jerky.

"Get 'em off!" a voice comes from below him.

Olly dive bombs towards the floor until he is floating sideways across the room.

Harry is dancing on one of the tables, repeatedly performing his infamous right-hand explosion. Benjamin is sucking up ice-cream through his gas mask straw.

"Are you okay, love?" the voice comes.

He looks towards the gramophone, but its lips are no longer moving.

"Olly, are you okay?"

Landing back in the chair with a painless thud, he sees Janet's twisted face of concern and big arms reaching towards him.

"No, I feel weird. I think I need to go home now," he replies.

"It won't be long now," she comforts. "He's on his way."

"Who? My dad?"

She smiles and turns her attention back to the scantily clad old lady and the white figure in the wheelchair.

Edith is reaching behind her back, giving the audience a cheeky grin and battering her eyelids.

"Edith! Edith!" the chants come. "Edith! Edith!"

An out of time drum roll fills the room as Edith milks the crowd. He can see buttocks lifting off chairs and hear the subsequent flat notes that emerge, as though the build-up of excitement is too much for them and needs to escape.

Finally, Edith rewards the audience for their patience and flings the bra to the left of the stage with dramatic finesse. Her breasts flop onto the head of the wheelchair occupant with rather less grace, but the crowd erupts into raucous cheer, nonetheless.

Darkness falls as the lights go out.

"Quite a show, Edith. Quite a show! Let's hear it once more for the lovely Edith!"

"More!" some of the crowd shout in protest.

"No. There are children present. Let's have some decorum, shall we?"

"Piss off, Rodney!" someone heckles.

The lights are turned back on. Edith has left the stage.

"I'll ignore whoever said that," Rodney comments, giving the first table a rather stern look. "Okay, before the main event begins, we have a special bonus act tonight."

There are murmurs of excitement across the room.

"Let's hear it for Ivy!"

People begin to stand, clapping with deafening volume. Olly's head feels like it's going to explode, and he has to put his hands to his ears to bring some mercy. He is struggling to see the stage, so he takes a sidestep to the right and arches his neck. *Where is she?* There's no movement. Through his pocket, Olly begins to strum the case of his mobile cover. The dizziness is coming and going in waves, but now it feels as though he is sinking into the floor, and he keeps lifting his feet to avoid being swallowed.

Edith sits back at the table, fully dressed, giving him a quick smile and joining in with the rapturous applause. Still no sign of activity, but the ovation shows no signs of letting up. Only as Olly's nana finally steps onto the stage, dressed in a stark white robe, does the crowd sit and fall into an unprecedented silence.

He watches her begin walking towards the wheelchair, something swinging around her neck. The arms of the robe appear to be joined as if she may be about to pray.

She looks to the crowd before moving her mouth to the microphone. "Page forty-six, please."

Judith shuffles one of the red books across to him and nods. As he picks it up, the first thing he notices is just how heavy it is, leading to his first conclusion that it might be a bible—like the ones on the show Trevor mentioned. He opens the book on a random page to find several strange symbols and the picture of a man tearing pieces of himself off. Some of the shredded skin lies on the floor next to the man's bony feet—a mass of wrinkled pink, covered in hair, warts, and oozing sores. The new flesh underneath is smoother and without blemishes.

Olly flicks across to page forty-six to find more of the unreadable lettering, and this time, the picture of a man bleeding on the ground, surrounded by others lapping from the puddles on the floor. It's unlike any of the bibles he's seen.

Attention back to the stage, Olly observes his nana speaking in a tongue he has never heard before. He can only assume she is reading a passage from the red book as he observes the others, their heads tilted down towards the pages. She speaks firmly and slowly, not like a nana, but like someone that has performed this many times before. They all say something in unison and snap their books shut, placing them back in the centre of the table. Olly places his on top, letting out a nervous shudder and longing to be far away from the old.

The lights go out once more.

Olly strains his neck and lifts his feet out of the quagmire to try and get a better position, squinting his eyes as if that will make a difference. Unnervingly frequent lightning basks the stage, creating its very own spotlights. It's as if the storm is right on top of them now, creating an almost permanent vibration through the floor and tables. He watches his bowl ever so slowly move towards the centre of the table and also notes the other bowls moving to join it, all in contrasting directions. The sight makes him dizzy again, and he reaches for the edge of the table for ballast.

There's an overwhelming sensation to shout to his nana that he wants to go home, but he refrains, praying for the night to end. He watches her bow her head towards the figure in the wheelchair. The others follow, eyes fixed towards the ground.

Silence falls. Only the faint sound of Benjamin's breathing can be heard above the rumbling of thunder outside. It's an eerie feeling after the room being so voluminous, and after a while, Olly finds it unbearably overwhelming, as though enormous pressure is building inside the room. White light continues to outline his nana's frame and the now seemingly rigid body beneath her.

He turns his attention to the person standing at the next table. Something moving in her hair—he's sure of it. Fixing his gaze, he watches as the grey curls continue to be disturbed. He quickly glances around to see if anyone is noticing this, but they're all oblivious, heads down. There it is again. This time, something begins to emerge, though, and under the flash of clinical white light, he notes the glistening darkness. More grey hairs give way as it pushes through, finally sliding down the woman's back until it falls lifelessly to the floor. No heads turn; nobody says a thing. He watches as the woman takes a step back and kicks it under the table.

Olly's normal life seems so distant, and he finds himself longing for routine. Only a few hours have passed since turning into Newhaven Crescent, but it feels as though the longer he spends here and the stranger things get, the less chance he has of returning to normality.

"Sit, please," his nana sternly says.

In unison, people quietly take their seats once more, maintaining their eerie silence.

"Thanks for joining us today, my amazing friends. And thanks for making my Olly feel so welcome."

Heads turn towards him. Smiles break out across the faces of all but the lady with the white hair. Olly focusses on her, deeming her the least crazy of the bunch, and even after the other heads have turned back, they continue observing each other. It feels like she's trying to say something to him, transmit her thoughts across. He has that sick sense again and wants to hide in the lady's candy floss hair until all this is over—when he can finally go home to his street populated primarily by middle-aged people with kids. Quite happily, he could spend the rest of his life without seeing anyone over the age of sixty.

"Are you with us?" Nana Ivy says.

There is no reply. Olly begins tapping the case of his phone again.

A series of lightning strikes illuminate the community centre room once again, but this time, frame a large shadow that appears on the left-hand wall. Olly stops tapping, but his heart picks up the pace he set. As the almost instantaneous thunder rumbles through the floor, he scans the room for the source, but everyone is seated and motionless, staring at the sinister silhouette on the wall.

"Janet," he whispers.

"Shh," she hisses back.

A shiver runs down his spine as Olly watches the shadow, frame by frame, making its way from the back of the room towards the stage. The form is tall and thin, with a large jutting out chin and small horns emerging from the head. Its long spindly arms swing slowly by its side, giving way to claw-like hands that are home to fingers resembling age-old icicles. Olly's skin crawls as the stage becomes immersed in even further darkness. More flickers of lightning highlight the shadow of the stranger that now towers above his nana. *Is she smiling?*

He watches the sleeves of his nana's robe separate and notices something in her right hand—*what is that? No—*

An impossible hot breeze rushes across his face.

She raises the knife high above her head. "This one is a gift, Master. He really got my goat!" She brings the blade down into the centre of the white bundle.

"Nana!" Olly screams, but there is only applause and laughter as the body begins to writhe like a worm once more and as redness begins to pollute the purity of its white cocoon. She brings the knife down again. And again. Finally, his nana steps away and bows her head.

A smoky haze begins to emerge from the carnage, spiralling rapidly in tornado-like fashion. Olly watches, mouth hanging open as the swirling mist begins to drift upwards towards the head of the shadow on the wall. With a flash of lightning and a heavy crack of thunder, both disappear.

Disbelievingly, Olly surveys the room, and all he can see are inane grins and twisted faces. Their laughter echoes in his head as they each turn to observe him. Faces spin around each other, teeth bite down, sores leak their vile blackness, and more glistening globules are birthed from necks, ears, and hair. As Olly feels himself freefalling through the madness, the room begins to spin. *I'm going to pass out.* But he can feel hands on him and bony fingers all over his shoulders and legs. The ceiling is rushing by in a blur. He closes his eyes and opens them, but there's no reprieve. Half-a-dozen faces bear down on him, but they are milky and out of focus. He is being hoisted up now and made to stand. Everything continues to swim in and out, but he can make out the blurry outline of the body in the chair and the blurry faces of the audience.

Someone grabs his hand. *Nana.* She leads him to the side of the wheelchair and whispers, "We look after our own," in his ear. He looks down to see multiple patches of red spreading across the white bandages and begins to feel queasy. Perhaps it's all just a bad dream, he thinks. Perhaps he's actually already in bed at Nana's house having a weird nightmare brought on by the cider. He really fucking hopes so.

He watches as his nana takes hold of a loose end of the dressing, beginning to unveil whoever is underneath. Geoff waves his box eagerly from his table, and Ivy nods her approval. He rushes onto the stage with a pair of scissors and begins unwrapping from the bottom up.

There's a tuft of hair coming through the top of the bandages. Black.

Olly's legs cave beneath him, and he reaches for the handle of the chair, accidentally brushing his hand against the bandaged head. Geoff snips eagerly at the toenails, collecting the shrapnel that falls to the floor and adding to his collection.

A pair of blue eyes are unveiled next. *It's him. It's Roger.*

"No, Nana," he mutters wearily.

"It's okay, Olly. Nana knows best."

Olly's legs finally give completely, and he falls to the floor in a heap. Darkness swims in, quickly drowning out the sympathetic smile of the lady with the white hair.

"OLLY," the soft voice floats across.

He opens his eyes, but it's like peering through frosted glass. His head is pounding, and there's a dull pain running down his right side. Finally, his eyes begin to settle, and he's pleased to find the room no longer spinning.

"Are you okay, Olly?"

"Is it morning? Can I go home?"

"It's Clementine, Olly."

"Who? Oh no, am I still here?"

"Olly, I want to talk to you before they finish preparing." She glances back to the others as they move the tables and chairs to the side of the room.

"Preparing for what?"

"The main event. And after that, your initiation," she says.

"What? What are you talking about?"

"They're going to bring you into the coven, Olly. You are blood, and to her, that is everything. She always looks after her own."

"I don't get it. I'm so confused. Why did they kill Roger?"

"Your dad told Ivy about him. He wasn't part of the plan, but Ivy knows best."

"My dad? He's part of this, too? No! No way," he says, shaking his head. "I don't—I can't take any more of this. My head!"

"They're going to sacrifice someone else tonight, Olly—a child, someone your age. Do you understand?"

"The paperboy, the one the officers were talking about? I can talk to her—to Nana."

"You don't understand, Olly. Your nana is the matriarch of this group. Do you know what that means? You've just seen her stab your mother's lover to death. You've seen what she is capable of."

"I've seen some things lately. Weird stuff. I just need to close my eyes and wake up properly."

"No, Olly. This is real. As real as it gets." She reaches for his hand and looks him in the eye. "I joined this coven thirty years ago when I was seventy-six years old."

"That's not possible. I mean, you're old, yeah, and you smell, and your skin is weird in places, but there's no way you're over a hundred."

"I'm a hundred and seven years old, Olly." She lifts a hand to her cheek and scrapes at her skin until loose flaps begin to hang down next to her chin. "I was weak, you see. Cancer was eating me from the inside. She said she could fix it for me, take it all away as she did for herself."

"This is too much," Olly cries, burying his head in his hands.

"Olly, will you please hear me out?"

He shakes his head vigorously, wrapping his arms tightly around his legs. Finally, he looks up into her watery eyes.

"I wanted the cancer gone so badly, Olly. The pain was driving me insane, but I wasn't ready to die—to leave my children and grandchildren. She asked Alf and me to meet her here at the centre, said that it was a decision we must both agree on before moving forward. He was so sceptical, but he came anyway because he loved me. I have to live with that, and much more."

She pauses to glance across the room again.

"Ivy made us drinks, sat us down, and then told us everything. Like me, she had been diagnosed with terminal cancer, given only days to live. She told us that she wasn't ready to accept her fate, to leave the world and her only son behind. She doted over your dad—couldn't bear the thought of leaving him. Every night she prayed, but not to God, to the other one."

"The shadow?" Olly says.

She nods. "He has many forms, Olly. The point is your nana and George were churchgoers all their lives, but that couldn't save her. In and out of morphine-induced states, she started to try and summon him, pleading that she would do anything for a few more years. The pain turned her dark, Olly. It can do that to you. After a while, she started to sense something in the hospital—a presence. She would see shadows on the walls and feel a draught even when the windows were closed. Initially, she thought it was just death looming over her, ready to take her soul, but she continued the invoking, and one night the presence came to visit her—in its true form. It crouched next to the side of her bed and offered the necklace—told her that if she agreed to his terms, then it would be his gift—a conduit to channel life from others into her."

"What terms?"

"He would take their souls as part of the deal." She looks to the ground. "When your nana woke, she thought it had all been a dream or a side effect of the drugs, but then she saw the necklace on the bedside table."

"Like sacrifices, you mean?" he says, shaking his head, not wanting to believe.

"Yes, exactly. But over time, each sacrifice becomes less rewarding. Restoring life source is a bit like recharging a battery—the more you do it, the less charge it holds, so eventually, death is going to catch up with us anyway. You've seen what is happening to our bodies. Our organs and bones may be holding up, but our skin is decaying, and badness leaks from within. And the hideous smell, a constant reminder of our ultimate destination. That's why she chose the paperboy—hopeful that such a young sacrifice will carry a bigger reward."

"Did Nana kill him? George?"

"As he was reaching to examine the necklace, she grabbed his wrist and inflicted her pain on him, but all at once, and with such ferocity that his hair turned white and his heart stopped. She carries his ashes in that pendant."

"The same thing happened with you and Alf?"

She looks away. "I pleaded with him to consider Ivy's proposal, but he didn't want anything to do with it. I begged him, but how could he under-stand what I was going through? It's a survival instinct, Olly—the need to keep breathing. Ivy anticipated how Alf would react, which is why she put the sleeping pills in his tea. She put something else in mine that sent my head funny, and then she started to work her way inside my mind. She's good at that, manipulating; it's what she does. The drugs make it easy for her, and she has us all addicted to whatever black magic the Devil helps her grow in her garden. You have to understand, I was so confused, out of it, but she made me feel as though it would be the most natural thing in the world. She held my hand as I carved through his neck."

He suddenly feels like he's burning up, not a drop of saliva in his mouth. "And your cancer?"

"All clear on the next consultation. The doctor said I was a walking miracle."

"What about—all these other people?"

"Not one person in this room is less than one hundred years old, Olly. We all had our health issues, and she manipulated and worked her way into our heads. Any partners that didn't fall in line, well—"

She clears her throat.

"I suppose you can think of us as a single beating organism that feeds on the life source of others. By joining hands with Ivy, the necklace shares the time across us evenly. I've lost count of how many people we've given to him over the decades. As long as your nana is breathing, Olly, so are we. The magic will die with her."

"This is crazy. I just want to go home to my own bed."

"I know you do, Olly. But that's not going to happen. Here, have some water," she says softly, retrieving the glass from behind.

He greedily glugs it down. "Why don't you run away or tell the police?"

"Oh, Olly, don't you think I've thought about it—about ending it all? For all the guilt, I can't bring myself to do it. You see, the deal made means that when we finally die, he will acquire our souls too—and the thought of that terrifies me."

"So, why are you telling me then? What am I supposed to do?"

"There's nothing you can do, Olly. I just wanted to confess to someone, I guess; get it off my chest. I've felt so lonely of late."

"I need to tell Mum or the police. I need to tell someone—to stop this," he says, desperately fumbling for his mobile phone again.

"You won't get a signal down here, Olly. This is as close to Hell as you can get without being there."

He lifts the phone in the air, willing bars to appear.

"I'm so sorry, Olly."

His arm suddenly looks much bigger, almost as big as Janet's. The display on the phone looks weird, too; the colours and numbers all merging into one.

"No, you—"

He crashes to the floor next to the empty glass.

ALEX

MOMENTARILY, Alex stops struggling and listens to the approaching footsteps.

It was a boy's voice before; perhaps he's brought someone back with him. Nobody surely would believe it was rats. *Come on, open the door, please!*

The footsteps stop outside the room. He holds his breath and twists his face in hope. He hears a key rattling inside the lock, and his stomach churns at the dull click.

Oh, God, please.

Light begins to sneak into the room as the door creaks on its hinges, and when he sees the gas mask, a feeling of euphoria sweeps over him. *Benjamin.*

"I've come to break you out, kid."

Alex speaks his muffled thanks as Benjamin squeezes past him and begins to guide him out. "The enemy is everywhere, sport. Lay low and do as I say. Roger?"

It's a strange feeling. He loves his mum and dad immensely, but all he can think about is giving Charlie-girl a big squeeze and apologising for not taking her for a walk. He decides he's going to take her for a really long one in the morning.

"Uh oh, I think we've been spotted, sir!" Benjamin shouts as the wheelchair rumbles over the door strip. "Prepare for battle."

Alex takes in the view, noting the stage area with a microphone and stand. He's so confused but doesn't care as he's already thinking about home and what snacks might be in the cupboard. He knows he'll be able to have whatever he likes after such an ordeal—how could his parents refuse? More voices come from further down, filling him with a further sense of comfort. Perhaps they'll even put in the extra for Dragonland, he thinks. As Benjamin swings him around the corner shouting "ambush," and as Alex surveys the faces of the residents of Newhaven Crescent lined up in the centre of the room, butt naked and injecting each other's privates with long needles, he begins to wonder if this really is the great escape he was promised.

The gag is ripped from his mouth, and he feels the prick of the needle before he sees it.

IVY

SHE'S NERVOUS, always is in his presence, even though he's kept his part of the bargain to date.

Stepping out of the bloody cloak, she surveys the blotched atlas that is her skin. Even copious amounts of body mist can't mask the putrid smell kicked out by the ever-weeping sores. In a little over an hour, though, her skin will be smooth again, and the smell and discomfort will be gone. She opens the fire exit door and lets the cool air rush over her nakedness, enjoying the temporary relief from the maddening itch of her skin.

To Ivy, these sacrifices are just sustenance—like a healthy lunch, and everyone needs to eat. What's important is the wellbeing of her flock, her friends, her community. She's noticed how fragile and weak they've been looking of late—that's the only guilt she feels. But Alex is a fine young specimen that should see them good for a while.

It feels good having Olly with her tonight. Like Frank, he will soon become part of the flock, and in the time that she has left, she intends to make the most of the necklace. The magic will die with her—that's what her master said—and she knows she is wringing out only a slightly damp towel these days. Regardless, she feels so fortunate to be able to help them out this way.

When Frank was diagnosed with heart disease last year, it was her calling to mend her son. Such a good boy—took to it so well. It was never her intention to bring him into the fold, but fate steered him that way, and a mother does what she can for her son. And young Olly, to protect him from illness and keep him safe, there is no greater gift she can provide.

"We're ready, Ivy," Clementine's voice calls through the door. Such a lovely girl; struggled with it right from the get-go, though, not like the others. She remembers so clearly how she and Clementine stood hand in hand, cutting through Alf's neck with the knife—two people pledging their commitment to each other for eternity. That's essentially what the group is, a marriage of the residents; for better, worse, sickness and, more importantly, health. She knew as soon as she met Clementine's husband that he wasn't right for the flock. There were others that had to be seen off, too, but that's the circle of life, she supposes. It's always the one that isn't in pain, the one not fearing the claw of death each time their eyes close, who is the reluctant one, the sceptic. Shoe on the other foot, she guessed they would most likely do anything to milk a few more years.

"Coming," she shouts. Running her fingers across the necklace, she thinks about George and the sacrifice he made for their community. *It's what he would have wanted.*

She slips out of her bra and panties, kneels to the floor, and begins to beckon the master once again.

ALEX

As Benjamin wheels him down the middle of the line, Alex tries his best to avoid staring directly at any of the nether regions. He's doing well until the wheelchair catches Joan's ankle at the precise moment the lightning flickers illuminate the room. She turns, sporting a lady garden big enough to grow carrots. For a moment, he sees himself in there, hacking it all back and pushing a wheelbarrow full of crops around.

"Alex!" she shouts, snapping him back into relative reality. She extends a big hand and ruffles his hair. He turns away and recoils, but even in the dim light and from his peripheral vision, he can't help but notice the way her pasty boobs swing like giant pendulums. He imagines a big cuckoo springing from Joan's mouth at any moment, and the way he's feeling, he's ready to mount that mother-fucking bird and fly out of here. That panting again, fast and excitable. And there it is, the stream of wee running down her leg.

"Looks like rain," Alex says, giving a subsequent giggle.

Benjamin continues pushing him down the line.

"Hey, sport!" Janet calls out to him. She's injecting something into Albert's misshapen ball sack. His wiener looks to Alex like a small puppy curled up in an oversized bed. With his good eye, Albert graces Alex with a wink.

"Told you, son. You've got to take life by the balls," Janet comments, removing one of her hands temporarily to perform a salute.

Alex ducks as he raises his giant hand in return.

Further down the line, he sees Geoff waving the steel toolbox above his head. He tries not to focus on the thing between the old man's legs swinging from side to side and beginning to hiss at him. Glancing towards the ground, Alex finds his bare feet and the crudely manicured nails that now grace his toes. *Of course.*

"Hey, good-looking!" He knows that voice.

"Edith," he shouts. "Why is everyone naked?"

"Why are you dressed?" she replies with a snigger.

Hands continue to reach for him from all directions, and he sways in the chair as best he can to minimise contact from the impossibly long and grotesque digits. Finally, Benjamin stops pushing the chair and swings him around to face the front.

Looking dead centre between the two lines of drooping sore-infested but otherwise pale white buttocks, Alex notices the child slumped in a wheelchair next to what looks like a microphone.

"Who's that?" he asks, watching his arm as it floats ahead of him.

"That's Olly," Benjamin replies.

"Is he going to sing for us?"

"No, but you are."

"I can't sing," Alex giggles.

"Everyone can sing, Alex. You just need the right tune."

The lights go out, and as the scorching breeze blows through the room, his skin prickles. The people in front nervously shuffle themselves into perfect lines, feet together, heads bowed, and hands clasped in front of their privates.

"What if I don't know the words, Benjamin?"

"You will. It's amazing how quickly they come when the music starts playing. Now, rest your voice for a moment, Alex, and wait for the music to begin."

The ensuing silence makes him want to giggle. Relentlessly, he begins to chew on the side of his cheek, unsure of how long he can keep from breaking into explosive convulsions. He tries to focus on what he's going to tell his mates at school tomorrow, but as he runs through the story in his head, he realises he has more chance of convincing them he spent the night on a spaceship having metal rods thrust up his bottom. The thought prompts him to chew down even harder, and the bitter taste of blood registers at the back of his throat.

It's the increasing darkness that finally brings some discipline—that, and the sensation of another presence in the room. The air feels thicker at the back of his throat, and the faint but offensive stench of sweaty butt cracks is being replaced with something far more pungent, a smell more foul and gut-turning than anything he has ever come across before. He's suddenly feeling more present, more alert, and the numbing sensation that was making him feel quite weightless is slowly beginning to lift, giving way to unpleasant tingles across his skin and prompting a shiver.

In the distance, he hears a door creak and shut, followed by the sound of footsteps approaching from the corridor. As another flash of white spills through the side window, lighting up the stage, he turns his attention back towards the kid in the chair, wondering if they made him sing and thinking perhaps they killed him because he didn't hit the right notes. He quietly clears his throat as the footsteps get closer.

He recognises her immediately as she turns the corner. "Ivy?"

She shows no signs of acknowledgement as she makes her way towards the two lines, completely naked apart from the low hanging pendant that sits between her floppy breasts. Her face is different today. Usually, she's quite jolly, but there is a seriousness about her that doesn't sit well with Alex.

"The pie was awesome," he says hopefully, but her face still does not change. "Guess I ate too much."

The others keep their heads down as she begins making her way down the line. Alex shuffles in the chair nervously, still trying to think of a song from the radio that the old folk might know. Lightning strikes as she approaches, and hot air blows across her thinning hair that gives easily like freshly planted grass.

"Why am I tied up?" he asks. "And why was I locked in the storeroom?"

Her lips are drawn into a fine line and show no sign of breaking formation. As she draws closer, shoulders hunched and arms by her side, the others begin to join hands and spread out into a more circular formation.

"I really need to be getting home, Ivy. My parents will be worried," he pleads.

Another flash of white pours through the window and momentarily frames a large shadow on the left-hand wall. *What the hell?*

"I need to take Charlie for a walk, my dog. She gets edgy if I don't, you see." He pictures her, staring out the bay window next to his mum, ears up and panting anxiously, waiting for him to come home. He'd give anything to run his hands through that matted chocolate fur right now.

She's right in front of him. Reaching her hands towards the armrests of the chair, she crouches down and lets out an explosion of wind that would usually crack Alex up, but he feels no inclination to laugh.

"What's going on?" he asks softly.

"Community service," she replies.

She leans in and begins to sniff him from head to toe, finally letting out a long exhale of satisfaction.

It's the only thing he can think to do. He clears his throat one more time and proceeds to nervously destroy the first three lines of an Elton John number called "Rocket Man," the last song he remembers listening to in the car with his mum. He looks towards Ivy for a reaction, but she gives nothing back and simply stares in a way that he finds unnerving. Another warm gust blows across them, and he's again overcome with the feeling someone else is with them. And that stench!

"I can try a different song if you like," he suggests nervously, a solitary tear rolling down his cheek.

The impossibly long flicker of light frames the shadows in the room perfectly this time. Directly behind Ivy, thick horns like age-old branches sprout from a head that takes up half of the back wall. Against both of the side walls are what look like claws, and they're getting larger all the time.

Further darkness falls around them, and Ivy stands, giving his hair a quick ruffle, before disappearing behind the chair.

The group surrounds him in a circle now. He snaps his head back in all directions, but their expressions are blank and offer him nothing but dread as they begin to close in.

Alex opens his mouth to begin another song, but only a croak comes out, and as the circle gets tighter still, there's an unsettling realisation that he wasn't brought here to sing.

OLLY

SOMEBODY WAS JUST SINGING—A kid—he's sure of it. Unless he was dreaming. Perhaps this entire night is just a nightmare.

He manages to partially open his right eye, but his vision is blurry, and his eyelid feels impossibly heavy. Giving out a small moan, he lets his eye collapse shut. A thumping pain runs across his forehead, and his neck feels like someone's been sitting on it. He tries both eyes but quickly screws them shut again as the room falls into a strobe effect that reminds him of last year's school disco, discounting the naked old people stood in a circle, of course.

What the—

SLOWLY, he tries again, and this time manages to keep them open. *Holy shit!* It's a scene he knows will give him nightmares for weeks to come, possibly years. *What the hell is going on?* He remembers talking to Clementine, and then —*the water. Something in the water.* He spots the kid in the centre.

LIGHTNING FILLS the room once more, and his attention is drawn to the silhouette of a head against the far wall. What look like horns sprout from it. Something on the far walls, too.

The conversation begins to play back in his head. *The paperboy. Initiation. The Devil.*

He tries to move but can only manage a small flick of his leg.

They're whispering now. He holds his breath to try and hear what they are saying, but the words don't sound English. A warm rush of air rustles his hair and makes his skin prickle.

I don't want to go to Hell!

The kid is beginning to make a strange sound.

"Stop," Olly says, but it comes out as a dry rasp. He tries to move again and manages to adjust to a slightly more comfortable position, his neck singing out in both pain and relief at the change.

"Stop," he says again, louder this time.

The paperboy looks up towards him. "Help," he shouts.

The circle is getting smaller.

"This isn't right, Nana!"

"Please help," the paperboy cries.

The old people continue their shuffle towards him, and it isn't long before Olly can no longer see the poor boy's eyes from behind the sore-riddled flesh.

"No, don't!" the poor boy screams. "Please!"

Olly pushes against the armrests for support and manages to raise himself slightly. He forces a leg forward and takes a gamble that he will be able to stay upright, but his leg gives, and he collapses in a heap by the side of the wheelchair.

The boy launches into a guttural scream. Olly's never heard a scream like it. Not like the movie screams or the time the spider landed on his mum's shoulder—this is a wild cry he thought nobody capable of.

"I'm sorry," Olly cries, helplessly watching the savagery unfold.

Excited grunts begin to emerge from the group, but Olly hasn't even got the energy to try and block his ears. The kid's screams begin to dwindle to a muffled cry as the wheelchair rocks violently from side to side. The thought of the kid somewhere under that pile of flesh, fighting for his life, fills Olly with such sadness and anger. No way in Hell does he want any part of this. The grunts are getting louder, more frantic, and in contrast, the hopeful pleas become no more than a smothered sob that slowly dies to nothing. He sees something emerging—the same hazy gas he saw when Nana finished sticking the knife into Roger. It hangs in the air, above the group.

Olly shudders on the floor as biting and tearing sounds leads to a more primal groan from the group. Like a pack of braindead zombies, they huddle and feed on the child. The horrific frenzy lasts for minutes until the group begins to withdraw back into their wider circle, still twitching and manic, painted with the young boy's innards. He looks to what's left of the boy in the chair, faceless, no longer someone's child, but leftovers—*a meal on wheels for the old folk.*

An audible gust rushes over the top of Olly's head, and in the dim light, he sees shadows moving against shadows. *The Devil is here for the boy's soul.* As if to verify, the lightning casts the silhouette of the sinister figure on all four walls, and just as quickly, it disappears as the room falls into dimness once again. A roll of thunder works its way across the floorboards. The wind is blowing hard now, hotter and showing no signs of abating. Another flash shows *it* closer, leaning in towards the boy.

The dry heat of the wind continues to sweep over Olly as he keeps his eyes pinned on the wall, heart pounding and longing to be anywhere else. There's another flash of light, and the claws are out this time, digits extended towards the boy. Another strike and the floating haze disappears, as do the shadow and wind. "I'm sorry," Olly whimpers.

He watches his nana, first to break the circle, running her hands down the back of her legs. "Doris, we need this mess cleared up, please. Gerald, give her a hand."

"Let me get the nails first," Geoff chirps in.

"I feel so good!" Janet yells.

"I feel bloody amazing," Judith adds. "No pain. And my skin!"

"Oh, I'm even sexier than I was before," Edith comments, running her hands across her breasts and then through the hair of her lady garden.

"Edith, you are going to get it tonight," Harry says enthusiastically. "You all are. Let's have some mood music, Trevor."

Olly manages to push himself up on the one elbow that has feeling, but the move exhausts him. He has to find a way out—before the initiation.

He watches as the group begins to come together once more, but this time their hands don't reach for each other's hands; they are all over each other's blood-covered bodies—in all the places they shouldn't be. This is a different kind of frenzy and one that is making Olly sick to the stomach. It's not like he's never seen sex before; he stumbled across his Dad's porn collection once, but that was two or three young people at a time, not a group of oldies groping at each other's saggy privates. He recognizes the slow tempo music in the background as another of his mum's favourites—Sexual Healing, he thinks it's called. He eyes his nana, close to the middle of the group, two old men and one woman doing unspeakable things to her. He's never seen that smile on her face before.

The scene is a horrific opportunity.

Slowly and stealthily, he drags himself to the side of the room where it's darkest and begins to work his way to the door. The moans are getting louder, and there's an awful slapping sound that is "all kinds of wrong" as his mum would say.

He turns to see Doris and Gerald wearing arm-length gloves carrying what's left of the paperboy's body to God knows where to do God knows what.

"Oh, Norman, you dark horse," Edith says. "Yes, just like that."

"Never mind him, concentrate on getting your gnashers around this," Harry comments.

He wonders how they became so hard, so evil. They've just killed a boy, and now they're having sex in his blood. From the other side of the room, he hears the notorious box of toenails shaking. *Christ, they're all at it.* Flashes of lightning bask the room, and he stops dead, thinking he might be seen. Following the sound of the toolbox, he eyes Geoff, one hand on the wall, the other wrapped around his collection, giving it to Clementine from behind. Olly holds his breath—*can she see me?* She appears to be staring directly at him. There's no expression on her face, though.

Olly thrusts his right elbow ahead for leverage and pulls himself along. The noises are getting louder, and the groans more animalistic. *This fucking place is nuts.* Exhausted and with a feeling someone is trying to punch their way out of his skull, he drags himself closer and closer to the door. A horrifying thought rushes through his head, and he pauses to check his pocket. Relief kicks in as he runs his palm over the hard casing. As soon as he's out, he will make a call. Who to? His mum? The police? Clementine said his dad is part of it. Everything feels so murky in his head, the drugs still making him so groggy.

"Olly."

There's a strange sense of relief as the voice floats across. It's as if fate is taking over, removing the anxiety of decision making. He lets himself rest and places his head on the ground, watching Harry's ejaculate explode for real, all over Edith's blue rinse.

"It's going to be okay," his dad whispers in his ear as he hoists him to his feet.

"Why are you naked, Dad? Where's Mum?"

"It's okay, Olly. It's sorted. We're going to be okay now."

Olly's head hangs limply to the right as his dad helps him across to the wheelchair in the centre of the room, the one in the middle of all the sweaty heaving bodies and the one where a young boy was only recently smothered to death. Easing him gently into the chair, his dad gives him that look—the one he always does to try and make him laugh. But Olly's not breaking this time.

"It's your turn next, Frank," Edith says, wiping the sticky liquid from her eyes.

"Not tonight, Edith," he replies.

His dad bends down and brings his lips within an inch of Olly's right ear. "Now, this next bit is going to get a bit weird, Olly," he says, "but it's worth it, trust me. If it wasn't for your nana and the kind folks of Newhaven Crescent, I'd be dead by now. What I had is genetic, son. Your mum doesn't want you to know, but I feel it's right that you do. Do you understand? Nana can protect you."

"But Dad, they killed a child. My age. A kid!"

"But how many lives will continue to flourish, Olly? That's one life for many."

The tears explode. "This is crazy. Please, can we go home?"

"I'm sorry, Olly. Your nana and I decided it would be for the best."

"I don't want to," Olly whimpers. "I want to go home. Can we please just go home?"

"Olly, you have to understand that Nana is just looking out for us. There's nothing more important to her than family—us and the rest of Newhaven Crescent. We're all in this together, and this magic—this gift—can make sure you live a life without pain. I would never want to see you suffer in any way."

"But I don't want to go to Hell!"

"Listen to me, Olly. We don't even know what Hell is like. Mum used to go to church every week, and for what—so she could spend months in bed, being fed through a straw? Our perception of Hell is based on horror movies. We have no idea what awaits on the other side, but surely it's wise not to take a gamble on this one—the one we are living in right now?"

"Take me home, Dad. I want to see Mum!"

"It's okay, Olly. It's okay to be scared. Nana put a little something together to help with your nerves. Just a little dose."

As Olly watches his dad bring the needle out of his pocket, he shrinks as far back into the chair as it will allow. "No, Dad. Don't! Please."

"Just think of it as a vaccination, Olly. Against everything."

Olly lifts his right arm in protest, but his dad easily swats it away and plants the needle into his shoulder.

"Dad."

"Sometimes, all you need is a little prick," Edith comments. "Isn't that right, Norman?"

"Cheeky bugger," he replies. It was twice the size in my younger days."

"A full inch?" she suggests, cackling. "Okay, who's next?"

Micky the Mime raises his gloved hand.

Olly watches his dad's face slowly shrink into a black dot. It takes off and begins to buzz around the top of his head, circling it numerous times. He tries to reach for it, but it's too quick and artfully evades capture. It loops a few more times before landing back on his father's neck and inflating itself back into the familiar head.

"It's going to be okay, Olly. Nana knows best," he says in a reassuring manner that has the opposite effect. He gives Olly's hair a quick rustle and makes his way around the chair. Olly turns, watching him walk towards the centre of the group where his nana is in the process of dismounting a very fogged-up Benjamin.

Everywhere Olly looks, flesh pounds against flesh in a series of gruesome frames highlighted by the relentless flickers of white light. Some faces are twisted in pleasure, some project boredom, and there are others that don't even look like they are enjoying it—as though providing a service. Huge fluffy speech bubbles hang above some of their heads, emphasising the sounds they're making—lots of vowels and exclamation marks. Clementine is still looking his way; he swears tears are running down her face. She doesn't have a speech bubble, but the word "Help" hangs in her cloud-like hair.

Slow-motion head shakes and floating hands indicate his dad and nana are in serious conversation. It continues for some time until his dad finally turns and bounces towards the stage. His nana positions herself at the front of the group and raises both arms in the air, speaking in that strange guttural tongue again. Olly watches intensely as her speech bubble fills with characters he's never seen before. The group dust themselves off and fall back into formation, adopting the pose of heads down and hands clasped in front. Silence ensues, and he knows the shadow will soon be with them.

Closing his eyes as another hot gust blows across his face, Olly finds himself on the beach, one hand up to his face to avoid the sand getting in his eyes and the other holding desperately onto the yellow plastic handle of a kite that twists and flips jerkily in the summer wind. From somewhere close, he can hear his mum's laughter drifting on the breeze. He lets the rest of the string out, but the tension is too great, and he watches as the kite snaps itself free and begins to drift erratically down the shoreline.

"Don't worry, Olly. I'll get it," his mum's voice floats in his head. Her laughter drifts into the distance as the sand ahead caves under her bare feet.

"It's just a kite. Leave it," his dad says. "He's too old for them now anyway."

It was their last holiday before his dad fell ill, and he has such fond memories of the laughs he and his mum shared. He wonders where that person has gone.

It's the sound of an approaching squeaky wheel that brings Olly back to the room. The familiar acrid smell is filling his nostrils—*he's here*. He turns to look at the group and finds them still in two lines, but with each of their heads drifting towards the ceiling like balloons. As lightning flashes outside, the balloons pop with an enormous explosion, deflating manically towards the ground until they connect with their rightful owners once again. Letting out a nervous giggle, he focusses his attention back towards the corridor, and even in the contrasting dim light, he recognises her red shoe immediately. *Mum.*

Just like the paperboy, she is tied up and gagged with tape, eyes wide with fear, and throwing herself around in the wheelchair, screaming muffled cries.

Olly tries to get up, successfully managing to plant one leg down, but the other isn't responding, and he flops helplessly back into the chair. "Mum."

"It's okay, Olly," his dad says, patting him on the shoulder. "It's all going to work out for the best."

None of it feels real, his head alternating between bizarre hallucinations and the gravity of what is unfolding. He watches his dad hand the blood-stained knife to his nana. The steel looks heavy and real.

"No, stop," he says, trying to push himself up. "You have to stop this, Dad!"

Desert-like wind sweeps across the room, and Olly senses the seemingly relentless hunger of the Devil.

"Son, she doesn't love us. She was going to leave us tomorrow for blue-eyed Roger."

"No, I don't believe you! She said you were trying to work things out."

Marching across to the chair, his dad roughly rips the gag from his mum's mouth. "Ask her," he prompts. "Let's see if she finds the courage for honesty for once."

Olly watches his mum take in a mouthful of air and looks into her desperate and watery eyes.

"Mum, is it true?"

"Olly, I love you. Always will, you know that." She gasps for more air. "Don't let them turn you against me!"

"You were going to leave us?"

A tear escapes down her already reddened cheek. "Him, Olly. I was going to leave him, and I promise I was going to come back for you."

"And the lies start again," his dad says, sealing the gag over her mouth.

"Can't trust her. It's you and me against the world, mate. But now we have an extended family—people we can trust."

All those times, his mum said they were trying to work it out, yet she was planning on leaving the whole time. He feels so betrayed. The fuzzy feeling is leaving, and he feels the anger-fuelled adrenaline running through his veins. It's making an audible fizzing and cracking sound in his head like sizzling bacon. He's taken back to the kitchen, laid out on the floor after falling from the chair, and his mum standing over him smirking—the day before she was going to leave. *How could she?*

"I HATE YOU!" he screams as he rushes towards her, legs solid beneath him for now. He starts bringing his hands across her face, and she turns in the chair to try and avoid the blows, tears streaming more mascara down her cheeks. He feels himself losing control, panting erratically, a combination of stringy saliva and his own tears hanging from his chin.

"OLLY, IT'S OKAY," his dad says, gently restraining his arms. The familiar smell of his dad's cologne helps to calm him slightly. "We don't need her, son. Your nana says we can move in with her when this is all over, become a proper part of the community. She's so excited about it."

"I'M SO CONFUSED," Olly utters. "This is all so crazy."

His dad crouches before him, but his naked form lends no sanity to the whole thing. "Something that saves your life can't be bad, Olly. I wouldn't be here talking to you now if it wasn't for these people."

"But the paperboy, Dad. I can't get him out of my mind. And Nana stabbed Roger—killed him."

"The only important people in the world, the ones we can trust, are here with us now in this room."

Olly observes the group as they begin to join hands and step back to form the now familiar circle. More lightning spills into the room and highlights the sinister head and sharp branching horns on the wall, along with the knife-like claws ready to reach towards another soul for the collection. The air is heavier. The stage is set for the Devil's work.

Stomach lurching, it feels like the floor is caving beneath Olly as he helplessly witnesses his world crumbling. The two people that he used to trust the most, the ones he thought had no secrets from him, have turned his world upside down.

Thunder explodes all around as his father grabs his hand and leads him into the group. Falling into line, he watches his dad coil his free hand around Nana's, the one holding the knife. Feeling weak and exhausted, part of him wants to close his eyes, but instead, he turns his attention back to his mum to find her face pulled back in terror as she relentlessly cowers in the chair, emitting near-silent screams. Another hand clamps around Olly's right wrist, and he turns to see a blank face bearing down on him. He surveys the rest of the group, only to find their features, too, being concealed by a new layer of skin quickly growing across their faces. Distressed, he turns to his dad, only to see his eyes disappearing behind a fleshy new veil.

Get a grip, Ol!

His head is spinning, and it's a battle to keep from passing out. He shakes his head but cannot make their faces reappear. What was it that Clementine said? A single beating organism.

Finally, Olly looks towards his nana. Her face has no such covering; she is the only one that can see—the only one that isn't blind.

She takes a step forward, and the rest follow in perfect synchronisation. As Olly is hauled along, he feels his left leg collapse, but his faceless dad hoists him up.

He looks towards his mum. Her muffled moans have stopped, and she is no longer squirming against the cheap plastic fabric of the chair. There's something other than terror now projecting from her eyes. The hot wind blows through her hair, and once again, he finds himself transported to the beach. He's looking through the crowd, scanning faces, but there's no sign of her.

As he's dragged along again with the circle, the vision is left behind.

"She doesn't love us," his dad's words echo in his head. The photograph of Roger pops in there, too. The smile, the stupid little lines above his nose. Mister perfect, ready to steal his mum away.

The group takes a step closer. Olly turns his face away from the heat of the breeze that accompanies their movement.

"Whore!" his nana calls out, spitting a ball of dark mucus towards the chair.

Another step forward.

"Heathen!" she hisses.

The circle is closing in, only a few feet away from where his mum sits, all fight gone and apparently accepting of her imminent fate.

Olly is swimming in and out; it's like he's watching a movie, but a sicker one than he's ever seen before. The circle is as tight as it can be now.

"Charlatan!" she shouts.

He watches his dad release his nana's hand. She takes a further step forward, raising the knife above her head.

"It really gets my goat!" she screams. The accompanying gust unbalances Olly, and he has to plant his right foot down behind him.

"Wait!" Olly shouts against the wind. "It's my mum. I should get to do it!"

She turns to him, knife hovering above her head.

"I hate her. Let me do it! Please, Nana."

He doesn't see anything behind her eyes, but she smiles and offers the handle of the knife. "You are your father's son," she says softly.

Olly pulls his right hand free and coils his fingers around the handle. Even before he lifts it from her palm, he can feel its weight, and the sight of blood on the blade only adds to its burden.

"It's okay if you can't," she says.

Finally, he takes the knife and waits for her to complete the chain. There's a gentle squeeze of his left hand by his faceless father.

He turns towards his mum and takes a step towards her, strengthening his grip on the knife.

"He has a special place for Jezebels like you!" his nana spits behind him.

Olly closes his eyes as another drift of heat ruffles his hair. Waves pound in the background, children run from the approaching tide as seagulls scout the sand for scraps, and old people lounge in deck chairs with handkerchiefs laid across their heads. "Get me an ice-cream, Olly." His dad's voice. And he sees her through the crowd, holding the kite high above her head, a huge smile plastered across her face.

The magic will die with her. The wind drops, the image fades, and he turns and sticks the knife into his nana's chest.

"She brought the kite back!" he screams.

There is no reaction, no cries, or acknowledgement of pain from his nana, just wide eyes full of shock. He pulls the knife out and thrusts into her again. "You're murderers!" Olly screams.

THE WIND GETS UP AGAIN, and his left hand is released. As hands begin to claw at his face and chest, dragging him away, Olly watches his nana drop to her knees, clutching at the wounds.

"My heart, Olly," his father mutters. "What have you done to my heart?" His skin is pulling back to reveal the features once more.

"I'm sorry, Dad. I love—"

"No, look at my fucking heart!" he screams, releasing his hands to reveal thick black veins snaking across his chest, writhing and slithering, spreading their darkness beneath his skin.

A series of moans sweeps across the group as they drop to the floor one by one. Bodies begin to spasm, arms flailing and legs kicking, their features being painted across their faces once more, albeit twisted and pained. The wind howls in all directions.

His dad looks across at him, squirming in agony on the floor. Olly can't hold his gaze, and as the sadness washes over him, he turns away towards his mum.

Over the incessant shake of toenails, the moans are getting louder and more desperate. Everywhere he turns, sores break out across limbs, and dark patches move under skin, some forcing their way out like moles, creating gaping holes that leak more of the thick glistening gloop.

"How could you?" Edith mumbles. "I thought we had something going on." Something worms out from between her legs. A huge mass of dark red matter the size of a tennis ball pulsates a couple of times before withering into black limpness.

He spots Micky the Mime gyrating on the floor in silent agony. "Fuck," Micky eventually mutters.

Lightning sweeps across the room and frames the Devil on all four walls— no doubt waiting to collect on the terms of the deal. It's been a good day for him.

Rushing over to his mum, Olly carefully removes the gag and turns his attention to her wrists.

"Quick, he's coming!" his mum shouts.

"I'll fucking kill you both!"

He turns back to his dad, who is now dragging himself towards them with the bloody knife in his right hand, face twisted in further betrayal. "I'm so disappointed in you, Olly."

"Fuck you!" Olly shouts. "Does that help? Fuck you!" Finally, he manages to get a fingernail into the crease and begins plucking at the tape.

"I did it because I love you," his dad snarls.

"Got it!" Olly screams as he rips at the tape.

With free arms, his mum instinctively reaches down, urgently beginning to work at her feet and giving out short, panicky breaths. "I've got nails. I'll get this!"

Olly turns around to survey the carnage and spots his nana, face down on the floor, still breathing, still holding on, while his dad is getting closer all the time, fuelled by rage and revenge.

"Hurry up, Mum!"

He can hear panicked breaths as she desperately claws at the tape. "I can't find the end!"

Shit!

His dad begins to push himself up, feet rubbing against the floor as he tries to get leverage.

"Mum!"

"I'm trying!"

"Fuck!" Olly screams, rushing over to where his nana lay in an ever-increasing pool of blood. He counts to three and slides his right hand under her head and over her mouth. "Sorry, Nana," he whispers. With all his might, he lifts her head back towards him and squeezes her nostrils with the thumb and index finger of his left hand. Her legs begin to slide weakly against the blood, and the surrounding moans turn to a unified lamenting wail. Olly looks across the sea of flesh that writhes against the floor, knowing they will be grieving for themselves and each other.

"How could you do this to me?" His dad is back to a crawl now, but it's slowing, and the skin is beginning to break across his back as though something is trying to escape.

"Looks like rain," Joan rasps as she gives up the fight and lays on her back, eyes fixed on the ceiling. Benjamin is taking loud and painful breaths, and Olly watches him struggling to raise his arms towards the mask. Finally, he manages to wrap his hands around it and slowly slide it off, revealing a glistening skinless mess. "I am your father, Olly," he says and gives a croaky laugh. He drops the mask and lets out a final long exhale.

"Any last requests?" Trevor asks.

"Witchcraft—Frank Sinatra," someone says.

And the remainder of the group begins to sing the tune with their last hoarse and raspy breaths.

Clementine lifts her head towards him and smiles. Perhaps this is what she wanted. She said as much that she couldn't bring herself to do it, and it was her voice in his head, "The magic will die with her."

He has to hope there was still some good left in these people.

Her hot breath against his palm is weak. A warm treacly substance runs down his fingers, and there are more pops and crackles as he feels her skin breaking down against his. He can't bring himself to look. His arms are killing him, but Olly wants to be certain; he's seen too many movies where the victim gets up for one last kill.

Beside him, Harry is on his back, wheezing for air. Olly almost feels sorry for him as he watches the guy raise his hand towards his wiener to give it a tug. He gets two in and opens his palm in a final orgasmic salute to the world before his head finally flops to the side, eyes as dead as stones.

Her breathing has stopped.

He keeps his hands there for a few more seconds just to be sure, but when he looks towards his dad's lifeless body, he finally lets his nana's head fall back to the floor.

Warily, Olly steps over to where his dad lies, and crouches, slowly prying the knife from his grip. "Sorry, Dad," he says, giving his hair a quick rustle. He takes it over to where his mum still sits, body rigid and fingers digging deep into the armrests of the chair. The blade works easily through the tape, and in seconds, he is peeling it away.

Helping his mum to her feet, they begin staggering towards the door that Olly entered through many hours ago. He turns to take one last look at the devastation around them. Bodies are beginning to fizz and bubble as skin cracks and bursts under pressure from the darkness inside. Everywhere he looks, there is badness leaking out, squirming its way across the ground until it fossilises and turns to clumps of dark matter.

The first of the bodies turns black, and the rest swiftly follow as though some form of super-mould is sweeping across them. There it is—the haze, leaking from them like a visible gas. In a series of cracks, the bodies begin to fragment into smaller pieces, eventually breaking down into nothing but ash. One final gust of wind scatters what's left of his dad and the residents of Newhaven Crescent.

He glances back to the door just as a bolt of lightning highlights his mum's washed-out face, but also the silhouette of the Devil on the wall waiting patiently to collect. The claws begin to reach out.

They were never cured; the Devil just put the disease on hold while they served him.

"Come on, Olly."

He wipes the handle of the knife across the bottom of his sweater and throws it into the centre of the room. "Coming!" He turns to go but glances back, thinking he might have seen something glimmering between the ash, near to where the knife landed.

Another flash of lightning explodes above their heads, and almost immediately, Olly can smell smoke.

"Olly! We've got to go!"

His mum swings open the door, and they both rush into the now rainless night, not stopping until they pass the sign for Newhaven Crescent. They finally rest, heaving in huge mouthfuls of air. They turn together to watch the building burn, huge orange flames lapping at the night sky that is now clear of storm clouds. Sirens blast in the background, but Olly is hoping they will be too late to save the place. He can still hear crazy bastards singing that song, though. *What was it? Witchcraft.*

"Can we bake tomorrow, Mum?" He begins to cry.

His mum takes him into his arms. "Of course, Olly. Anything you like," she says.

"Not cherry pie."

"Okay," she says, bringing him in even closer. "I love you so much."

"I know. How are we going to get home?"

"Have you got your phone with you?"

Olly reaches into his pocket and lifts it in the air. Three bars. He cries some more.

JENNY AND OLLY'S PLACE
SUNDAY, 2ND SEPTEMBER 2018.

HE WAKES up to find himself in his parent's bedroom, the sunlight sneaking through the side of the blinds. He reaches for his phone on the bedside table. 10:56.

Something feels different, aside from the obvious. He's watched plenty of movies about coming of age, his favourite being 'Stand by Me,' and while it was traumatic to watch, he figures those kids got away quite lightly, all said and done.

He can feel the pain in the pit of his stomach for the loss of someone he once idolised, someone that could make him laugh just by the flick of an eyebrow or wrinkle of the nose. Planting a foot down, he pushes himself from the bed, sniffing at the air as the smell wafts through. He feels guilty for feeling so ravenous. The mouth-watering odour gets stronger as he trudges down the stairs, and he can hear a humming emerging from the kitchen.

His mum is standing next to the oven. Pancakes are on the go. "Hi, darling," she says. He's glad to see that smile.

Beatrice jumps on the counter and runs her tail across his nose. It's a move that always makes him sneeze, but he has to admit, he's pleased to see the little shit this morning.

"Achoo!"

"Bless you," she offers.

"Thanks."

"What a night, eh?"

"Yeah. I guess."

"I thought we could do with a good breakfast."

"Pancakes—what people eat after choking out their nanas."

She laughs but almost immediately begins to cry, hands clenched around the counter. "It's going to be a long day."

"I'm so sorry, Mum."

"What for?"

"You know what for. All this time, I've been a dick—sorry—an idiot. I think when dad got ill, it got me scared, freaked me out, you know."

"Olly, it's okay. He was your dad, after all."

"Just let me finish, okay? Even before the illness, he was always just the joker, making me laugh. But I know it was you that kept it all together. The school stuff, the sports, the homework; I can see it now, but I didn't then. It's like I've just woken up, seen him properly for the first time."

"Thanks, Olly," she croaks, wiping away the tears. "How many would you like?"

"How many have you got?"

"Enough. And if not, I'll make more."

"I haven't cried for him yet, Mum."

"We will, darling. The good memories will hit us when we're least expecting them. Grief will do that. We have each other, though."

She flicks on the radio, and they listen to the end of the old tune play out over the crackles.

It's just like old times, him and his mum in the kitchen, hanging out. And the pancakes are good—so good—just what he needs. He knows there will be questions and fall-out, and they'll need to get stories straight, but for now, he's content being here with her. One thing is niggling him, though; the flash of silver he saw before they left—could have been his imagination, he supposes.

It's a beautiful day out there today folks, makes you glad to be alive, doesn't it? This next track is a slow one taken from the Marvin Gaye album, Midnight Blue...

ABOUT THE AUTHOR

Mark Towse is an Englishman living in Australia. He would sell his soul to the devil or anyone buying if it meant he could write full-time. Alas, he left it very late to begin this journey, penning his first story since primary school at the ripe old age of 45. Since then, he's been published in Flash Fiction Magazine, Cosmic Horror, Suspense Magazine, ParABnormal, Raconteur, and many anthologies, including the newly released Midnight in the Pentagram from Silver Shamrock Publishing. His work has also appeared three times on The No Sleep Podcast and many other excellent productions. His first collection, 'Face the Music,' has just been released by All Things That Matter Press and is available via Amazon, Dymocks, B&N, etc. His novella, Nana, is coming March 2021.

View his website at: https://marktowsedarkfiction.wordpress.com/

ABOUT THE EDITOR / PUBLISHER

Dawn Shea is an author and half of the publishing team over at D&T Publishing. She lives with her family in Mississippi. Always an avid horror lover, she has moved forward with her dreams of writing and publishing those things she loves so much.

D.&T Previously published material:
ABC's of Terror
After the Kool-Aid is Gone

Follow her author page on Amazon for all publications she is featured in.
Follow D&T Publishing at the following locations:
Website
Facebook: Page / Group
Or email us here: dandtpublishing20@gmail.com

f ⊙

Written by Mark Towse

Formatting by J.Z. Foster

Cover Art by Don Noble of Rooster Republic Press

Nana

·

Printed in Great Britain
by Amazon

79131143R00058